More
SCARY
STORIES
for Sleep-Overs

By Q. L. Pearce
Illustrated by Bartt Warburton

An RGA Book

PRICE STERN SLOAN
Los Angeles

10 9 8 7 6 5 4 3   ISBN: 0-8431-3451-8

Library of Congress Cataloging-in-Publication Data

Pearce, Q. L.
    More scary stories for sleep-overs / by Q. L. Pearce.

        p.   cm.
    Summary: A collection of eleven scary stories.
    ISBN 0-8431-3451-8
    1. Children's stories, American.   2. Ghost stories, American.
[1. Ghosts–Fiction.] I. Title.
PZ7. P61458Mo 1992
[Fic]–dc20   92-21705
                                                                    CIP
                                                                    AC

Designed by Michele Lanci-Altomare

*To W. J. P. — for opening the door ever wider when the beasties
and phantoms of these stories came to visit our home*
—Q. L. P.

*To Shirley Finnell, as always,
and to the other three B's—Brian, Brett and Babsie-Pie*
—B. W.

Contents

Swimming Lessons

oathsome water demons were the first things that Heather thought of when she saw the gray-green waves of Crocker Lake. Last evening, Heather's grandmother had told her favorite story about sea monsters that dragged people to their watery deaths simply because they could walk in the sunshine. Today she stood on the shore of a big, mysterious lake where her parents had rented a cottage for the summer.

The family, which included Heather's outgoing brother and sister, Andy and Amanda, would be staying there until school started. That was eight long weeks away. It wasn't that Heather was anxious to get back to school. It was this place . . . the lake. From the moment she saw it, she was eager to leave.

Heather's dislike of water was not new. She was the only one of the three kids who couldn't swim well. When she had been very small, her mom had taken her to the local pool for lessons. One afternoon, when she was running to join the class, she had slipped at the edge of the pool and flown headlong into the water. The impact knocked the wind out of her, and she had sucked in a huge mouthful of water before she surfaced. Choking and gasping, she had clung to the edge of the pool until the teacher helped her out. Since then she didn't feel comfortable in the water and managed to avoid swimming most of the time. Andy and Amanda, on the other hand, loved it. Andy was on the junior swim team at school, and last summer they both had taken junior lifesaving courses at the "Y." Nobody except Heather ever thought about the wicked sea monsters, waiting under the water for unsuspecting victims.

Each day at the summer cottage the three kids walked about a mile down the beach to a special spot that they had discovered, then Andy and Amanda swam out to an old raft anchored about fifty yards offshore. It was nothing more than a wide, thick wooden plank connected to two huge oil drums. Along the shore, Heather would build sand castles, collect shells, draw, read or sit with just her feet in the water and watch her brother and sister. They seemed to have lots of fun pushing each other into the deep blue water and racing from one side of the raft to another.

One day, as Heather sat on the beach and watched them play a noisy game of King of the Mountain, she had the odd sensation that something was observing her. The beach was bordered by a dense stand of scrub pine. Heather turned and squinted into the dark patches between the branches. Suddenly, she felt something in the cool water touch her bare foot. Like slick, slender fingers, it drifted around her ankle. She shrieked and fell backward, yanking her foot out, only to find that the "monster" was just a trailing water plant.

She jumped up and pulled the slippery, leafy strands away. Dusting off her shorts, she turned to find her sandals and bumped right into a scruffy-looking, bearded old man. She screamed again.

"Now, now, missy," the old man soothed, adjusting a pair of wire-rimmed glasses on his nose. "There's nothing for you to fear from me."

Heather felt herself trembling all over, but she didn't want to appear frightened. "Why did you sneak up on me like that?" she demanded.

He rubbed the stubble on his chin. "I don't rightly think I was sneaking up on anyone. I might be asking you, what are you doing on this part of the shore?"

"I don't see why that is your business."

"Well, actually it is. You see, I own this stretch of beach from the shoreline to the road. You can just see the roof of my house beyond those trees."

Heather blushed. She realized that the old man was probably Mr. Patterson. He took care of the cottages during the winter when no one visited the lake. "I'm sorry. I didn't mean to be rude. I hadn't expected to see anyone. You scared me."

"I don't blame you for being afraid," the man said.

"There's plenty to be worried about. But not here. Out there." He pointed his gnarled finger toward a small island near the south shore, overgrown with bushes and towering trees.

"What's the matter with it?" Heather asked. In the afternoon sun, the island looked harmless enough.

"Depends on who you talk to." Mr. Patterson eased himself down to sit on a large fallen log. He picked up a stick and began to draw in the damp sand, first a line to represent the shore, then a small circle to symbolize the island. Heather knelt in the sand beside him. "Oh, there's a real good reason to be careful of that place. You see, the way the tide has to squeeze in through here," he dragged the stick between the island and the shore, "it creates quite a current. At certain times of the month, it can be really treacherous." His voice took on a sad tone. "There's been an awful lot of accidents out there over the years."

Heather wrinkled her brow, and she said, "You mean people have died out there . . . drowned?"

"Oh, yeah. In fact, just last summer four visiting kids were drowned on the back side of the island, along with the two deputies who were trying to save them. It was real strange, though," the old man mused, shaking his head. "Alice Anne Taylor, one of the deputies, grew up around here and could handle a boat in almost anything. No one ever quite figured out how the current got the best of her. Some say there is more to contend with out there than just the current . . . much more. There's an old Indian legend that says that those who die in these waters never rest . . . they just wait and watch for others to join them."

Heather felt a shiver run up her spine. She thought of the tales that her grandmother told. She could almost hear the heavily accented words: "They envy those who walk in the sunshine. They drag them down to spend eternity at the bottom of the frigid water."

The old man continued, "But then, there never seem to be any witnesses. Last summer only the two empty boats washed ashore, and they weren't talking. So, it's best to just stay away from that place."

"Hey, Heather!" Andrew called as he stood dripping on the sunny beach. "Heather, c'mon!"

"I have to go, Mr. Patterson," Heather said, standing and brushing the sand off her legs. "Thanks for the warning."

The old man frowned. "See that you remember it."

• • • • • • • • • •

The following day the family had a picnic lunch on the shore. After carrying the dishes back to the cottage, Andrew and Amanda asked if they could go for a swim.

"I think it's too soon after eating," their mother fretted. "I'd rather you stay out of the water for a while."

Instead, the three kids took a walk along the beach, picking up shells and bits of twisted driftwood. They were well out of sight of the cottage when Andrew found an old rowboat.

"Hey, look at this," he said as he checked it for holes and cracks. "I think it's seaworthy. Here are the oars."

"Andrew," Heather cautioned, "Mom asked us to stay

out of the water."

"She meant we shouldn't swim," Amanda said. "I'd love to row around a bit. Maybe we could explore that little island out there. I'm sure she wouldn't mind that. Come on."

Andrew and Amanda started to push the small craft out into the water. Heather thought of Mr. Patterson's warning. "Please don't. It isn't safe."

"Of course it is," Andrew countered. "There's nothing wrong with the boat at all."

"It's not the boat!" she almost shouted. Her brother and sister stopped and stared at her. "It's the island," she added quietly.

Shading his eyes with one hand, Andrew glanced at the small body of land offshore. "What about the island?"

"Mr. Patterson said—" Heather began. "Well, he says the currents are too dangerous, but I think he was trying to warn me about something else, too. He said some kids drowned out there last summer, and it was really weird. There's an Indian legend about this lake. . . . "

Andrew glanced at Amanda, and a smile began to play at the corners of his mouth. "Oh, no, another legend. I think that crazy old man is just trying to keep everybody away because he has something to hide. Maybe it's treasure!" He pushed the boat farther into the water and leaped in. "C'mon!"

"What kind of treasure do you think it could be?" Amanda asked as she jumped in behind him.

"C'mon, Heather," Andrew coaxed. "It will be fun."

Heather didn't budge. Tiny wavelets lapped at her

ankles. "I don't want to. Please. We could do something else. Building a fort would be more fun."

Andrew tilted his head at her. "There's really nothing to be afraid of. We're all together, and we won't let anything happen to you."

Heather set her jaw in refusal.

"OK, if that's what you want." Andrew pulled away. "But we're going. You can stay here all alone if you want."

Heather opened her mouth to protest, but then she had the odd feeling again that she was being watched. She didn't want to stay alone on the shore or walk back by herself. Maybe her brother was right. Maybe it would be fun and she was letting her fears prevent her from enjoying her summer, and after all, she wouldn't actually be in the water. If they were all together, it would be OK. She took a deep breath and climbed into the boat.

At first, Heather thought that her worries were unfounded. She actually started to relax. Andrew handled the boat well, and there wasn't much of a current at all.

"I'll bet there is a treasure chest filled with jewels on the island," Amanda fantasized.

"If I were a pirate, I would have hidden my loot there. Avast, mateys," Andy sneered at his sisters. "Head straight for that patch of land yonder or ye'll be walking the plank."

Amanda laughed. "We don't have a plank, dummy."

Heather giggled, too. This really was fun. Andy began to sing a song that he thought might befit a pirate, and the girls joined in as the mainland shore dropped farther away behind them.

As they approached the island, however, things began to

change. Although it was early afternoon, the sunlight appeared to fade. Without warning, the wind picked up and so did the current. Andrew fought the oars as the tiny boat was swept along.

"Amanda, help me."

"What do you want me to do?" Amanda was trying to be brave, but she could hear the nervousness in her brother's voice.

"Take one of the oars and just try to hold the boat steady. I think if we swing around the back side of the island we can ride out of it." He aimed the bow of the boat toward the small circle of land.

"What can I do?" Heather asked. Her brother was showing signs of tiring.

"Watch the shore. We have to get around that point, and we don't want to get in too close."

Heather did as he asked. When they rounded the point, she was the first to see the "people" standing among the tangle of vegetation that extended from the small strip of beach into the water. They looked almost human—as if at one time they had been. They seemed to be standing, not in the water, but on its surface. Whatever they were, they were gazing directly at the children.

"Andy!" she cried out. "Who . . . what are they?"

For a moment the three sat in stunned silence. Then Andrew found his voice.

"Row! Row as hard as you can!" Both Andy and Amanda heaved at the oars, scrambling to get away, but the boat edged closer to the dreadful island. As Heather watched helplessly, several of the horrid creatures slipped

beneath the surface. Then, from under the water, ghastly pale hands reached up and grabbed the edge of the boat, rocking it from side to side. Amanda stood and beat at them with an oar. She was the first to plunge in. Andy reached out to grab her and toppled over the side. Heather tried to hold on, but it was no use. She felt the boat tip . . . felt herself sliding into the water . . . the frigid grip of icy hands. Even underwater she could see the grisly chalk-white skin. The creature pulled her down, closer and closer, until she was looking into its deep-green, lifeless eyes. Its long, black hair drifted around it in floating, twisting tendrils.

Somehow Heather broke free, fought her way to the surface, and gasped in a lung full of air. Screaming and kicking, she sensed herself being lifted from the water, then pulled aboard a boat by warm, human hands. It was Mr. Patterson. She tried to speak, to tell him that Andrew and Amanda were still out there, but no words came.

As his motorboat turned toward the mainland shore, Heather noticed that the wind had dropped. There was no current, and the island was completely deserted. She felt as if she were in a dream. Mr. Patterson took her to his cabin and wrapped her in a warm blanket.

"I'm so sorry," he said as he handed her a cup of hot tea. "I saw the three of you rowing out. I tried to get to you as quickly as I could, but the motor on the boat—I couldn't get it started. These old hands are so clumsy."

Heather looked at his hands, the same hands that had pulled her from the water. "Did you see them?"

"Your brother and sister? No, I was too late."

Heather looked into his eyes. "Did you see *them*?"

The old man sighed. "I didn't see much of anything once I came around the point. Like an old fool, I was in such a hurry. I was trying to do too many things at once. My glasses—well, they slipped into the water. I couldn't see much of anything. Still can't. Everything up close is pretty blurry. I was lucky I found you."

They sat without speaking for a moment until a harsh buzzer broke the silence. Heather jumped. "That's the deputy," Mr. Patterson reassured her. "I called the sheriff's department. I'm afraid I can't see well enough to drive you home, and it's beginning to get dark. After what you've been through, I don't think we should walk. They've already called your parents." He adjusted the blanket around Heather's shoulders, and they stepped outside into the twilight.

The female deputy slipped her arm around the girl. "You've had a terrible shock," she whispered softly. "You're all right now."

Still stunned by all that had happened, Heather didn't even look up. Mr. Patterson squinted at the deputy in the gathering darkness. "Her folks are over at the Ames place. You'll be sure that she gets there safe and sound? Poor little thing, I wish I could take her there myself, but. . . . "

"Don't worry," the woman assured him. "You've done all you can. I'll see that she joins her family right away."

Nodding his head, Mr. Patterson patted Heather once more on the shoulder and turned back to his cabin. Heather let herself be guided down the lane toward the place where the deputy said her car was parked. After a moment she became aware that they were moving past the dirt road and toward the lake.

"Where are we going?" she demanded. "This isn't the right way." As she twisted away, the blanket slipped from her shoulders. Heather felt the deputy's icy hand. Looking up, she saw that the woman's long, dark hair was wet. In the moonlight, she could see the horrible green eyes and a tarnished name badge on the uniform that read TAYLOR.

With her last reserve of strength, Heather bolted away, running until her heart felt that it would burst. She didn't realize that she was still heading for the lake until she slammed against something cold and damp and fell to her knees.

"Where are you going, little sister?"

"Andy! Amanda!" Heather cried out in relief. "Thank goodness, I thought—it was so horrible—I thought you both had drowned." She gazed up happily at her brother and sister as they leaned toward her in the gloom. "How did you—?"

Her relief seeped away and was replaced with mounting terror as she realized that Andrew and Amanda, dripping wet, were staring down at her with lifeless green eyes.

"No! Oh, no!" Heather wailed, trying to shrink away from them.

Grinning, her brother wrapped his clammy arms around her as her sister said, "C'mon, Heather, it's such a nice night for a swim."

Wish Fulfillment

reg was the only fifth-grade student who didn't like his teacher, Mrs. Reed. But then, Greg didn't seem to really like anyone. He thought her classes were too boring and didn't hesitate to mention that to anyone who would listen. Even when the teacher arranged special events, such as a visit by a real astronaut during a class on the solar system, Greg criticized the idea.

Now that the mummy and certain belongings of the great Egyptian pharaoh Tutankhamen were on tour, the class was scheduled to go on a field trip to the local natural-history museum. All of the students were excited about the trip . . . well, almost all.

Greg started complaining as soon as the class began to board the bus that would take them into town.

"This is dumb," he grumbled to Maria, the girl unfortunate enough to sit next to him. "Who wants to see an old dead guy?"

Maria scowled. "I do. King Tut was one of the most famous people who ever lived. When he was our age, he ruled a whole country. I think this is exciting."

Greg waved his hand. "That's not such a big deal. When I grow up, I'm going to be famous, too."

"Oh, yeah?" Benny Taylor twisted in his seat to look back at Greg. "What are you gonna do to become famous? Talk everyone to death?"

"I've got a plan," Greg lied. "I haven't absolutely decided yet, but there are a lot of things I could do. Maybe I'll be a race-car driver." He looked at his companions to see if they were impressed. No one was. "Not just any old race-car driver," Greg continued. "One of those daredevils like the guy that jumped over the Grand Canyon."

"Nobody ever jumped over the Grand Canyon!" Benny snorted.

Greg crossed his arms and smiled smugly. "Then I'll be the first one. You'll see. Someday everyone will know who I am."

Benny and Maria both laughed as the rumbling of the bus engine grew louder and the vehicle carefully turned out of the parking lot and onto the main road.

Greg might not be very enthusiastic about visiting the museum, but he was pleased to miss a day of school. He really didn't see the point of learning history and geography.

Those kids that work so hard and always turn in homework and stuff are dumb. There's an easier way, Greg thought to himself.

The drive to the city took less than an hour. During that time, Mrs. Reed explained to the children that the museum was fairly large so it was important that they all stick together. She informed them of the rules that they would be expected to follow, such as being as quiet as possible and not touching any of the objects. Finally, she passed out a map of the museum to each student. The room that held the Egyptian exhibit was marked with a large X.

Soon the yellow school bus pulled slowly into the parking lot in front of the city museum. Talking and laughing, the children filed out of the bus and gathered at the entrance to the building. Near the door, a beautiful fountain spouted a glistening stream of water into the air. The morning sun created a breathtaking rainbow that quivered in the delicate spray. Greg barely noticed it. He simply whined about how hot it was standing in the sun.

"When are they going to let us inside?" he griped. Once inside the huge, air-conditioned lobby, he continued to protest. "This is going to take forever. When are we supposed to stop for lunch? This is so boring."

Finally, Maria had had enough. "Look, Greg," she said angrily, "if you're going to do nothing but complain, you're going to ruin it for everyone else. Why don't you just keep your comments to yourself?" She walked off to join the rest of the group.

Greg watched her go. He hated it when someone told him to be quiet. "Go ahead, jerk. I didn't want to come anyway." The other students turned a corner, and Greg slowed down enough to find himself alone. He had decided to explore on his own when Mrs. Reed peeked back around the corner.

"Gregory, please stay with us. I don't want to have to worry about you."

Grudgingly, Greg trailed along as the group passed by a display of early American Indian art. As he reached out to feel a large woven basket, a nearby guard spoke up.

"Please don't touch that, son. It's very old."

"So what?" Greg responded and looked defiantly into the man's eyes.

The guard was obviously irritated with Greg's lack of respect. "Why don't you stay with your teacher, kid? You might get into trouble roaming around on your own. And don't touch anything!"

Greg was about to say something in return but thought better of it. He sauntered away, unsure which direction his group had gone. He turned back to ask the guard but found himself completely alone. The marbled hall was curiously quiet. Dark-toned paintings in gilded frames lined the walls. From every direction, painted eyes stared at him. Greg could feel their gaze, and it made him uneasy. He headed toward the far end of the hall.

Moments later he found himself before a grand archway marked "The Tools of Ancient Magic." Carefully, he pulled the crumpled map of the museum from his pocket to see how far he was from the Egyptian room. Oddly, the tools of ancient magic exhibit did not appear on the map. Still, it sounded a lot more interesting than hanging around gaping

at a moldy old mummy, so Greg stepped through the arch and found himself in a spacious room.

The light was mainly provided by small spotlights over the displays. Against each wall was a tall glass case presenting unusual objects made of wood, rock or bone and decorated with beads, feathers and shells. One sign identified a large, carved bone as an object for casting out evil spirits that cause mental illness. A small crystal was labeled as a charm that would protect the wearer from poison. But Greg was drawn to a lone exhibit spotlighted in the center of the room. It was a huge, rough rock at least ten feet tall. Some long-forgotten person had carved it to look like a human face with long earlobes and a jutting jaw. The rock was surrounded by velvet ropes. A sign stood nearby requesting that visitors not touch the display.

For a moment Greg stood in front of the sign, then he smiled and reached out to run his fingertips over the stone. It was surprisingly warm and soft, almost like human flesh. He trailed his fingers along the side of the wide, silent mouth.

"Ouch!" he cried as he snatched his hand back from the rock. Something sharp had pricked his finger. A tiny drop of blood glistened at the corner of the statue's lip. Looking around to be sure that he was alone, Greg reached out to rub the drop away, but he only caused it to smear. He felt the stone grow warmer, and the air around him seemed to hum. Greg's heart raced. He quickly whirled and dashed for the door, but it was gone! Turning completely around, he saw that there was no exit, just four smooth, solid walls. He threw himself against the place where the door had been, but it didn't budge.

"Hey! Hey! What's going on here?!" The terrified boy pounded at the wall with his closed fist.

"What do you want?" a deep voice echoed behind him. Greg froze. Fearfully, he turned to see a shadowy figure standing near the statue. "I asked you what you want," the voice repeated. "Why did you call me?"

"I didn't call you," Greg stammered. The dark bloodstain glittered on the stone.

"You did."

"I'm sorry," Greg was trembling. "I didn't mean to. I was just . . . I just wanted to get out. . . . "

"Let's get it over with!" the figure interrupted. "It's bad enough that I must use my powers for the benefit of worthless humans. I don't need to listen to your meaningless babble as well."

As frightened as he was, Greg bristled at the insult. "Who's worthless? Who do you think you are?"

"I know precisely who I am," the being answered. "I am a genie of the most ancient realm."

Greg's amazement and curiosity overpowered his fear. "A genie? You mean like from a bottle?"

The genie seemed very annoyed. "Something like that. Now what do you want?"

"You have to grant wishes, don't you?" Greg's terror had turned to pleasure. This was it! He had always known something like this was going to happen to him.

The genie sneered. "It seems you have done a little reading. I'm overwhelmed by this display of intelligence."

Greg was losing his temper. "I wish you would stop

being so mean and just give me an answer!"

The light dimmed. For a second the surroundings grew hazy, then became crystal clear.

"Yes," the genie said smugly. "I must grant you three wishes. One down and two to go," it snickered. "But be careful. Fortune sees to it that no one gets any more than they deserve."

"You tricked me out of one wish," Greg frowned. "But I'm too smart for you. I know exactly what I want and now you have to grant my wishes." He stood proudly with his hands on his hips. "I want to be the richest boy who ever lived. And I want to be famous—one of the most famous people in the world." Once again the room dimmed and details swirled into an indistinct pool of color and shadow.

When things became clear again, Greg was lying on his back. All of his classmates were gathered around him in awe. Maria leaned in close. He heard her whisper, "Wow."

Benny stared steadily into his eyes. "Cool."

Greg felt triumphant. He tried to open his mouth to shout, "I told you so!" But nothing happened. Struggling to sit up, he realized that his body wouldn't respond. The only thing he could feel at all was a deep, penetrating cold, the cold of the grave. His nostrils were filled with the smell of countless centuries of decay.

Mrs. Reed leaned over Greg. She was smiling. "Yes, children, the boy king was the richest of the pharaohs. During his short life, he was probably one of the most important people on earth. You might say he was the richest, most famous boy who ever lived."

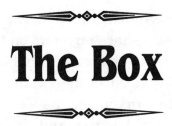

The Box

"eady or not, here I come." Tad uncovered his eyes and looked around. In one direction he could see a carpet of short, spiky saw grass that seemed to roll on for miles. Sunlight glinted off the standing water in which the grass grew. On another side, tall, spindly cypress trees rose from soggy flatlands dotted with shallow pools. Tad was standing in the cool shade of a thick stand of pine and live oak. At first glance he seemed to be alone, but he knew they were all there. His two little sisters would be the easiest to find. They never went very far into the swamp, and they always giggled. He saw a flash of red off to his left. He turned in that direction, treading cautiously. His dad had told him that's how Indians moved. The only Indians Tad ever saw were those selling souvenirs on the Tamiami Trail, but he loved Indian lore and read everything he could about the people who first lived in the swamp. His father knew lots of Indians. He worked for the Central and Southern Florida Flood Control District, and probably knew more things about this land than anybody.

A twig snapped a few feet away. Tad eased up to a half-rotten, moss-covered log and leaned over it. Two small girls were crouching behind it, heads close together, hands across their mouths stifling laughter.

"I see you!" he whooped. The girls squealed and ran off in the direction of home base. It was no contest. He tagged them easily and declared them slaves. They would have to wait there while he searched for Dave and Scootch.

Tad headed out into the swamp. There were probably a few snakes around and maybe even a gator or two, but it was pretty safe and easy to get around since much of the swamp had dried up. In the fall, the ground he was walking on would be knee-deep in mucky water. Because of the danger, he wasn't allowed to play out there then.

An Indian legend claimed that strange spirits lived in this part of the swamp. Tad had seen pictures of ancient rock carvings and paintings from the area that showed scenes of odd, green-eyed, long-faced creatures falling to earth from the stars. Tad's mom said there were enough hazards out there without worrying about ghostly aliens.

A rustling noise caught Tad's attention. He stood perfectly still. The sound was coming from a pile of brown leaves fanned around the base of a palmetto tree. Slowly, he crouched down to pick up a small stone. Aiming carefully, he threw it. A few dried leaves crackled like tissue paper, and a long, mustard-colored lizard broke cover. Tad pounced, grabbing it behind its neck. The little creature squirmed in his hand. That was when he heard Dave calling his name. He'd forgotten all about the game. He gently released his captive and watched it scurry to safety.

"I'm over here!" Tad yelled, cupping his hands around his mouth. A moment later two boys tumbled into the clearing. They were panting hard, and both tried to speak at once. Dave finally forced the words out between gasps.

"We found s-some-somethin' . . . out there. You gotta come see." Scootch just nodded as he tried to untangle his shoelaces.

Tad figured this must be really important. "What is it? A body? Indians?"

"Uh-uh, better," Dave whispered. He leaned in and said, "It's a secret passage."

"C'mon, are you kiddin'? Way out here?"

"I swear!" Dave raised his left hand. He wasn't too bright and would have to stay back in the fifth grade at Clewiston Elementary this fall, but when he vowed something was true nobody questioned it.

"OK," Tad grinned. "Let's go." The sun was directly overhead when the trio reached a wide hammock covered with cypress and scrub pine. Even in the brightness of day, dark shadows huddled under the trees, shadows from which unseen eyes could track the boys' progress deeper into the swamp. Scootch pointed out some puma tracks leading off into the dense undergrowth. None of them had ever actually seen a wild puma before, but at night, safe in their beds, they'd all heard the snarls of the hunting cat.

Before long they came across the remains of an unlucky armadillo. "I don't like this place. I think we're too far out," Scootch murmured, eyeing the body and looking, around. "Maybe we should forget it."

"Nah, don't worry. That cat is long gone." Tad tossed a clod of dirt at the armadillo. A cloud of flies rose, then settled again.

"C'mon. It's over here," Dave said as they skirted the carcass. He led the way up a wide mound. It was only a few feet higher than the surrounding area, but that would be enough to keep the patch of land above the water level when the rains came.

Tad poked around in the thatch with his foot. "There's nothin' up here," he huffed. Suddenly, he felt himself falling. His leg slipped through the tangle up to his thigh. There was nothing but open space under his foot. He scooted back to solid ground. "Wow! What is it?"

Proudly, Dave pulled at the matted vines. "I did the same thing. That's how we found it. Look." A large clump ripped free. Tad stretched out on his belly and gazed down into the black gaping hole. The cold damp air stung his nostrils. Something was down there, something very old.

"Wanna go down?" Dave poked at him. "I have my penlight."

"We don't know what's there, Dave. Besides, there's no way to get down." Tad desperately wanted to investigate the opening, but he knew that the swamp held many surprises and exploration could be dangerous unless they were properly prepared.

"Uh-huh. See, there are some kinda stairs." Dave shined his light on crude stone steps descending into the blackness.

"What about the girls? I left 'em alone, and they don't know where we are," Tad said feebly. He knew he was cornered.

"They'll be OK. They'll get bored waitin' and probably go home."

"All right, but leave Scootch up here to stand guard in case we need help." Against his better judgment, Tad agreed.

Dave nodded, and Scootch sighed with relief. The two boys lowered themselves into the opening. Dave went first with the flashlight. It was difficult to keep their footing on the damp, slimy steps.

"Hey, Scootch!" Dave yelled up. "Try pullin' away some more vines." Dried leaves, grass and small twigs showered down on them as the boy tugged at the thatch above their heads. With a crackling sound, a large knot of it gave way and sunlight streamed into the pit.

Their surroundings took shape around them. The passage was about six feet across and the steps, which were carved directly from the stone, curved about fifteen feet toward a small opening in the opposite wall. Whatever this place was, it had been here for hundreds of years and the swamp seemed to be trying to reclaim it. The walls were green with mold, and moisture was seeping in on all sides.

"I wonder why this doesn't dry up like everything else," Dave whispered.

"It's probably below the water line. Limestone's real porous." Dave furrowed his brow at Tad. "How'd you know that?"

"My dad told me. Sometimes he takes me out on field trips, as he calls 'em. We do experiments and stuff. This whole place is nothin' but sand, mud and limestone."

Finally, they stood before the opening at the base of the steps. Dave shined the flashlight inside the passageway but it didn't do much good. "Are you with me?"

Tad tried to keep his voice steady, but he had an uncomfortable feeling. He wanted to turn and get away from that place as quickly as possible, but his curiosity was stronger. "Sure," he said. "Let's go."

They ducked under the arch and found themselves in a small, shallow cave that at first appeared empty. "Be careful," Tad cautioned. "There might be water moccasins." Dave nodded and moved on, his sneakers making squishing noises in the foul-smelling slime. He swept the light in a back-and-forth motion across the floor.

"Tad! Look at that!" A few feet away a massive rectangle of stone rose out of the reeking muck. It was very wide, nearly shoulder height, and about seven feet long. It appeared to be topped with an immense slab of solid rock. The sides were deeply carved with intricate figures and designs, some familiar . . . most not.

"This is an Indian place," Tad murmured. "It looks like an altar or somethin'."

"You mean for sacrifices?"

"Or a tomb . . . I don't know."

"Look!" Dave pointed his tiny light at a wide depression in the rock. Nestled in it was a smooth grayish box, about the size of a shoe box. It was wreathed with shells and stones. "What is it?"

Tad tiptoed closer. "I don't know for sure. It looks like it's made out of some kind of metal. It sure isn't something that the Indians made. But those are strings of rutoo shells around it. The Seminoles thought they were magic and used them to trap their enemies in one place."

"You mean the Indians trapped something in there—like an animal or something?" Dave backed up a step or two. "How did they know it wouldn't get out?"

"The legend goes that the shells contain the spirits of dead ancestors. The spirits are responsible for keeping the enemy in place, but they can do that only as long as the strings of shells are unbroken. Whoever put this here sure used a lot of them." He cast a sidelong glance at his friend. "They must have been terribly afraid of whatever was in that box. They used some powerful medicine to keep it there."

"Let's take it," Dave breathed.

Tad could feel his body shaking. He wanted to do just as Dave suggested, but somewhere deep down inside some primeval fear gnawed at him. "We really shouldn't move it."

"C'mon, you don't really believe in all that magic junk," Dave said, even though he was too afraid to pick up the box himself. He looked at Tad and said slyly, "I bet your dad would be real proud of you for finding this."

It was true. Tad knew this was the sort of thing his father had been searching for on all of those field trips. Dave pushed him forward. "Go on. Take it!"

Trembling with fear and anticipation, Tad reached out and gripped the box. But then, when he tried to lift it, it seemed glued to the spot. Closing his eyes, he tugged harder. Abruptly, the rotted strings that held the rutoo shells gave way, and he stumbled backward. Something unseen brushed against his foot, then slithered away in the ooze. A bone-chilling wind swirled through the cave. Suddenly, it seemed as if a thousand voices were whispering a single warning, a warning that Tad sensed rather than heard.

"No! Don't free them!"

As impossible as it seemed, it felt as if hundreds of phantom hands were tugging at his fingers and grasping helplessly at the box. In the darkness he saw that the container was beginning to glow. It felt slightly warm in his hands.

In terror, Tad lurched forward to return the frightening object to its resting place. But he knew it was too late. The ancient magic that had confined it had been undone. The rutoo shells crumbled into dust, and the huge stone slab began to slide away, revealing that the massive stone beneath was hollow. Inside, there were what appeared to be two large, coffinlike cylinders. They were made of some strange glassy material and filled with swirling, unearthly greenish gas.

Rooted to the spot, the boys watched with dread as a seam along each cylinder popped open, and the tops raised slowly in a cloud of medicinal-smelling gas. The penlight slipped from Dave's grasp and sank in the muddy puddle on the floor. Still, an eerie glow from the now-open stone illuminated the cave as slowly, ponderously, a silver-suited figure rose from each cylinder. Raising what looked like bizarre laser weapons, the beings turned to look directly at the boys. They had long faces and large, emerald green, catlike eyes. One of the creatures lifted its hand toward Tad and bared its sharp, ragged teeth in some sort of grin. Although it didn't actually speak, Tad understood it.

"The box," it seemed to order. "Give me the box."

As if waking from a trance, Tad turned and careened, slipping and sliding up the steps, out of the hole and back into the sunshine, with Dave at his heels.

Scootch was at his side, babbling. "What'd you guys see down there? What'd you find? What is it?"

"Run! Get out of here!" Tad screamed. "They're right behind us!" Dave was about halfway out of the pit when a green flash of light crackled up from below and enveloped him. For one moment he looked down at himself with a surprised expression, then at his friends. The next moment there was a sizzling sound, and Dave was gone. The smell of charred flesh filled the air.

The beings appeared at the opening and leveled their weapons at the two remaining boys. "Let's go!" Tad yelled. Dropping the box, he sprinted farther into the swamp. A bolt of green light hit the ground to his right. A large patch of vegetation glittered, then disappeared. Behind him, he heard Scootch shriek, followed by that hideous sizzling sound. Staggering, he regained his balance and raced deeper and deeper into the swamp. Tad didn't think about the snakes or the gators or the approaching night. He pushed everything from his mind but the thought of escape. He didn't even realize that he was no longer being followed.

• • • • • • • • • •

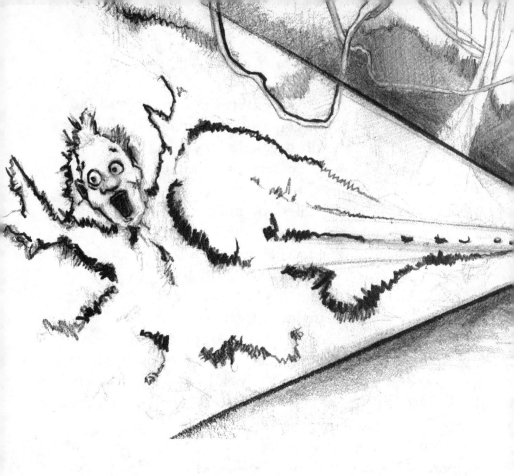

At the opening to their former tomb, one of the creatures knelt, carefully lifted the metal box and opened it. Inside was a maze of tiny wires and a keyboard covered with peculiar symbols. As he held it, a light began to speed along the tubes, and a low humming sound vibrated the box. He fingered a few keys, then motioned to his comrade, who was watching Tad disappear into the endless sweep of saw grass.

"Let him go. I've sent our position. It won't do him any good to run. Besides, we should be grateful. Because of his primitive curiosity we have finally gained our freedom. We underestimated the earthlings last time and allowed

ourselves to be captured while we were in our energy pods. This time, we'll take no chances."

● ● ● ● ● ● ● ● ● ●

Beyond the orbit of Pluto, the sleek star cruiser was nearing its destination when they first picked up the signal.

"Captain, we're picking up extreme emergency signals from Solar G3 in this system."

The captain blinked his large, emerald green, catlike eyes. "Do we have a team there?"

"Yes, sir." They were stationed seven hundred planetary years past."

"That's a world of very primitive civilizations. Our team should have taken over by now! Something must have gone very wrong. Arm all support crafts. Seal the quadrant! Set hyper-light speed. We're going in with full force!"

• • • • • • • • • •

Far away, Tad collapsed, exhausted, across an outcrop of rock. He rubbed his scraped and bleeding knees. It seemed as if he had been running for hours. In the distance he heard the growl of a hunting puma. "It'll be OK," he tried to convince himself. "I'll circle back tomorrow and warn my dad. He'll know what to do." There was nowhere he could go until morning, so Tad rolled onto his back and took comfort in watching the stars. He fell asleep without noticing the dozens of points of light in the night sky that seemed to be growing larger and coming closer . . . and closer.

Green Thumb

here are you going, young lady?" Mrs. Guerrero held up her hand as Leah headed for the door.

"I'm going with Dad. They're judging the entries for the tomato-growing contest today. I want to get a look at the competition, so he's going to drive me to the fairgrounds early."

Her mother shook her head. "You know very well that you are going to win that contest just like you have for the past three years."

"Hope so!" The girl raced to the kitchen door and grabbed a home-baked muffin as she sped by. It was still warm from the oven.

Leah scrambled into the passenger seat of her dad's red pickup.

"All set?" he grinned.

Leah nodded, her mouth full of food.

"After using that special soil mixture you've worked up, your tomatoes this year are better than ever." Her father pulled the truck out of the driveway and onto a narrow dirt road that led to the highway.

Leah agreed. "It really worked well, but I think I've come up with a few things that will make the plants grow even bigger and faster. I've added them to the old compost pit over behind the stone wall at the far side of the house. Is that OK?"

"I don't see why not. No one ever goes back there," Mr. Guerrero said as he turned the pickup onto the main highway.

• • • • • • • • • •

The following morning Leah was up bright and early. First she put out a bowl of milk for Jake, her orange-and-white-striped kitten. Then she proudly added her new blue ribbon to the others displayed in a glass cabinet in the living room.

Later, she and her mom cleared a large patch near the barn for pumpkins. Leah spread a thick layer of her newest soil mixture over the area and worked it in thoroughly with a hoe. After lunch she rode her bike to the store to pick up some things for her mom.

"Hi, Leah." Mr. Warden, the grocer, looked up as she came in. "Your order is ready, and I have something for you." He handed her a magazine. "This came in a pack of seed catalogs. It was the only one, so I think it was a mistake. Anyway, it's about exotic plants. You might find something special in it for your garden."

"Gee, thanks, Mr. Warden." Leah slipped the gift into her grocery sack. When she got home, she curled up on her favorite window seat with the magazine. Jake padded gently along the sill and stretched out in the sun beside her.

A small ad on the back page caught her attention. "What's this?" she said to herself. The kitten looked up as if waiting for her to say something more.

Guaranteed to amaze, it read. *The world's most unusual vine. Only for the most accomplished of gardeners.* Leah was intrigued and challenged. She filled out the little coupon provided and posted her order that very day.

Less than one week later, a small box, addressed to Leah and simply marked "seeds," arrived in the mail. She quickly opened it, ripped the top from the packet inside and tapped a few light, dainty red seeds out into her hand.

"What are they?" she asked aloud. The instructions on the packet just said to sow them near the surface and fertilize with bone meal. Leah got permission from her mom to plant the unusual seeds in a part of the area they had cleared for the pumpkin patch.

Within two days, the first pale shoots showed themselves above the rich soil. Within a week the plant was several inches high.

"Wow, Jake. Can you believe this?" Leah crouched down beside the young plant and rubbed one of its bright green leaves. Long, slender tendrils curled out from the stem. "I've never seen anything grow this fast. Except maybe you."

Jake wasn't particularly interested. He had discovered a small hole in the ground and was busily trying to excavate whatever had made it. Leah straightened up and looked at her chubby kitten. He turned his attention to a cricket, slapping at it with his paws. One well-placed blow stunned the insect.

"Good boy. You keep trying. I hope you turn out to be a natural ratter. You'll have plenty to keep you busy if you do." She headed for the house, then stopped short. Had she heard a soft sigh? "It must have been the wind," she said to herself. Behind her, a threadlike plant tendril snaked out and wrapped tightly around the motionless cricket. Jake laid his ears back, bared his teeth and hissed as the slender stalk dragged the tiny body into the soil.

•••••••••

During the summer Leah usually slept with her window open. She liked to fall asleep listening to the sounds of the night. One evening just as she was drifting off, she heard a strange but familiar sound. Opening her eyes wide, she listened carefully. It was a soft, wistful sigh, almost a moan. Where had she heard it before? Rising quietly, she crossed to the open window and tried to peer into the dark. A sharp squeal pierced the night, then another. Both came from the garden. Once again everything was still. "It sounds like rats," she said under her breath. "Jake must be on the prowl."

From then on, Leah heard the fearful squeals every night. Each day she tended her peculiar plant, which seemed to grow more lush by the hour. The barn wall was nearly covered with long, twining tendrils. Trumpet-shaped, bloodred flowers covered much of it, and she counted eight long, gnarly seed pods hanging from the highest vines.

One morning she decided to add more of the treated "miracle" soil from her compost pit around the plant's roots. Leah's mind was not on her work, however, as she dug her hands into the ground. She was worried about Jake. He hadn't shown up for breakfast. Leah had already planned to search for him when she felt a slight sting. Yanking her hands from the thick, dark brown earth, she watched as a droplet of blood formed at the tip of one finger.

"I should have been wearing gloves," she mumbled, wondering what might have caused the small cut. Looking down, she noticed that the end of a single root protruded just above the soil. The pale, greenish point was smeared with a tiny bit of blood. Leah touched it lightly. It was sharp. Suddenly, the root seemed to quiver, and it moved slightly toward the blood on her cut finger. She drew back her hand and jumped up. "I think I've been working in the sun too long. I'm letting my imagination play tricks on me," she reasoned.

•••••••••

"That treated soil of yours certainly speeds up growth," her mom commented over dinner that night. "I used just a little in my azaleas, and I could swear they have shot up a foot in less than a week. I can't imagine what an entire potful would do. It's certainly done wonders for your new plant, too. I don't think I've ever seen such a healthy vine."

"Thanks," Leah responded, but she was still a little troubled. She couldn't shake the feeling that there was something evil about the strange vine.

Her dad added, "I think our little Jake deserves a round of applause, too. He's turned out to be quite a ratter. I haven't laid eyes on a single rat in the barn for more than a week. By the way, where is he?"

"I don't know, Dad. I haven't seen him since yesterday. I looked for him all afternoon," Leah said worriedly.

"That's odd," her father mused. "Come to think of it, a lot of pets have been reported missing lately. Liz Bersen told me her boy's pet goat wandered off a couple of days ago, and they haven't seen it since."

Her mom patted Leah's hand. "I'm sure he's all right, dear. Cats can take care of themselves. He'll be back."

"I hope so," Leah murmured.

When Jake didn't show up the next morning for breakfast, Leah was certain that something was wrong. She decided to look for him once again in the barn. They had no livestock, so the barn was used mainly for storage. It was a perfect hiding place for rodents and thus an ideal hunting ground for a clever cat. The old wooden door screeched as she entered the cool, dark building. The only other sound was that of her own footsteps on the hard-packed earth.

"Here, Jake. Where are you, boy?" There was no response. Her dad was right; there were no rats anywhere. In fact, there seemed to be no insects either, nothing living . . .

except. . . . Scanning the base of the wall, she saw dozens of curling, green tendrils growing in through the cracks. In a darkened corner, one strand was wrapped so tightly around something that she couldn't quite make out what it was. She walked to the spot and nudged the vine with her foot. The limp tail of a very dead rat protruded from within the coil. Leah felt the hair rise on the back of her neck. There, near the body, was Jake's empty, blue collar. She edged out of the barn and backed into the garden. As she moved near the vine, she felt something lightly touch her leg. "J-J-Jake?" Lifting back a wide leaf, she was horrified to see a thick plant tendril shoot out and twine around her leg, tightening all the while.

"Dad . . . Dad!" she screamed with all her might. In no time her parents were beside her. "It's attacking me! Get it off! Get it off!" Her father quickly sliced through the stem with a pocketknife.

"Leah, what happened? Calm down."

"The plant," she sobbed. "It's the reason there are no rats. It got Jake, too. I know it."

Her mother stroked her hair. "That's not possible, dear. It's only a plant. You just got tangled in it somehow. But if it worries you, we'll dig it up."

"And burn it?"

"If that will make you feel better."

Within the hour, Mr. Guerrero had unearthed the plant. When he came into the house, he smelled slightly of smoke.

"Did you burn it, Dad?"

"Yes, honey. I burned every leaf, every flower, and all of those weird seed pods." He decided it was best not to tell

Leah about the collection of small bones he had uncovered at its roots.

That night Leah lay awake in her room, straining to hear the dreaded sound. Her parents had already gone to bed when she heard it, but it was not where she expected. The noise came not from the garden near the barn, but from the far side of the house, beyond the stone wall about thirty yards away . . . the area where she had so carefully tended her large pit of treated soil.

"Jake?" she sat up. "Maybe he really is OK. Maybe he just ran away, and now he's come home," she reasoned.

Slipping on her pair of slippers, Leah crept downstairs to the kitchen. She reached for the flashlight that hung near the door and stepped outside. It was a dark, moonless night. She pointed the flashlight toward the ground to light her path. All the while she softly called, "Here, kitty. Here, Jake. Come on, boy."

Pebbles scattered as Leah climbed over the crumbling stone wall on the far side of the house. A gentle sound, barely more than a moan, made her freeze in her tracks. Stunned, she lifted the flashlight. Its beam illuminated a huge vine that was part of a gigantic plant. It grew directly from the deep pit of special soil and covered the entire wall. Before Leah could open her mouth to scream, a slim tendril slid around her throat. Its leaves covered her face. The flashlight clattered to the ground.

The flashlight's beam of light slowly faded as dawn approached. A gentle breeze rustled the strong, healthy vine growing in the shadows. At its crown a long, gnarly seed pod suddenly split open, just as one had a few days before on the parent plant. The breeze lifted the small red seeds inside the pod and carried them aloft, scattering them in every direction.

Nightmare

odd was in a hurry. He planned to meet his friends Paula and Charles at Levy's Drugstore after school. Today was delivery day for new magazines, and he was anxious to get a copy of the latest *Monster Madness*. It was a double issue and included the details for a drawing contest that Todd wanted to enter.

Todd was a true and faithful fan of fright. Frankenstein, Dracula, the Werewolf, the Creature from the Black Lagoon—Todd knew all of the stories in complete detail. Ghost stories were good, and he wouldn't turn up his nose at an alien adventure, but tales of monsters were his favorite. The scarier and more gruesome they were, the better. His notebook was filled with drawings of sharp-fanged, drooling beasts stalking through darkened streets, searching for unsuspecting victims.

By the time he arrived at Levy's, his friends were already perched on the bench outside of the store. Charles was working the monster maze, a feature that always appeared at the end of the magazine. Paula, sipping a soda, was deeply engrossed in a story. Todd quietly leaned his bike on its kickstand and crept up behind his friends.

"*Yeeaghhhhhh!*" he roared.

Both kids jumped. Paula dropped the can, and a small, fizzy brown puddle quickly formed on the sidewalk.

"Jeez, Todd, you scared me to death."

"I'm sorry," he said sheepishly, picking up the container. "I'll buy you another soda."

"No, that's OK," Paula grinned. "It was warm anyway." She held up her copy of *Monster Madness* and pointed to the cover. The illustration was of a very tall, thin, scaly green beast, covered with green, slimy algae. Its skinny arms reached well below its knees. It had left a dripping trail from the lake to the door of a cabin—a cabin that probably housed unwary human victims. The title read, "The Creature from Luckless Lake." "There are some great stories this month. Isn't this guy the creepiest? It's enough to give me nightmares for a week!"

Charles rose to his feet. "Nah, my favorite is the alien brain beast. Talk about nightmares!" He held the magazine open to a drawing of a hideous, bug-eyed creature. Exposed at the top of its enlarged head was a huge, greasy-looking brain laced with blood vessels. "Could you imagine coming face-to-face with this guy on your next trip to dreamland?"

Todd laughed nervously. He had been having some unpleasant dreams lately. Although they were unsettling, he had decided not to tell his parents. His mom didn't like him reading things like *Monster Madness*, and if he told her about the nightmares, she would stop him for sure.

To cover his own uneasiness, Todd chided, "Yeah, and think how scared that brain beast would be if he got a look at you!"

Giggling, the kids strolled into the drugstore. Todd picked up his own copy of the magazine and counted out exact change at the register. He leafed through it as they walked out into the waning afternoon sunshine. They all lived on the same street, five blocks away. Todd wheeled his bike along as they headed home.

"So which one do you think is scarier?" Charles asked. "The brain beast or the lake creature?"

"I don't think either one is very scary," Todd replied. "I could make up something better than both of them put together."

Paula rolled her eyes. "OK then, what kind of monster would you make up?"

Todd thought for a moment, then began to describe his ultimate terror: the creature that had been haunting his dreams lately. "First of all, it would be about my size."

"Oh, c'mon," Charles interrupted. "What's scary about a midget?" He was always good-naturedly kidding Todd about being the shortest boy in class.

"Don't laugh," Todd shot back. "Because of its size, the monster can hide in shadows and get very close. It could even hide in the shadows of your own bedroom."

Charles and Paula looked at each other. The sun was nearing the horizon. The shadows of the trees reached out toward them like long, dark fingers.

"Its size wouldn't matter," Todd continued, "because it would have super strength. It could rip your arm from its socket without any trouble at all."

Paula suddenly stopped. She was searching the branches of a low hedge just ahead of them. "Did you see that?" she asked.

"No, what?" Charles's voice was a little uneasy.

"It was dark and furry, sort of like a big dog or a bear or something."

Charles chuckled. "C'mon, there are no bears around here."

"That's right," Todd chimed in. "There are no bears." He knew he was making his friends nervous, so he made his voice as spooky as possible. "And it probably wasn't a dog either," he said, although he was certain that it was. "It had thick, brown fur, didn't it, Paula?" She nodded, her eyes growing wide. "And if you had gotten a better look, you would have seen fiery red eyes and long, shining claws."

A rustling sound in the bushes made the three walk a little faster. Even Todd was getting anxious now, but he had the full attention of his audience and wasn't about to give it up. "The only thing longer and sharper than the shadow monster's claws are its teeth. Oh, and one other thing: it has a long, rough tongue for stripping meat from bone so that it doesn't leave behind a single scrap." Todd felt particularly pleased with that detail. He had read that lions had rough tongues for such a purpose, and it seemed to work well for his monster. It was certainly effective. Both Paula and Charles grinned uncertainly.

"We'd better hurry up," Charles said. "It's getting dark." They covered another block in no time, and Todd waved good-bye to his friends. He jumped on his bike and rode the last half block alone. As the shadows lengthened, he became aware of a strange sound. Something like a light tapping or scraping noise. He turned and looked behind him. There was nothing there. Still, he pedaled a little faster toward his house.

· · · · · · · · · ·

After dinner that night Todd did his homework, then got ready for bed. His parents always allowed him to read for a little while in bed, and tonight he used the time to finish two of the stories in *Monster Madness*. When his mom and dad came in to tell him lights-out, his mom picked up the magazine and leafed through it.

"I'm really not sure you should be reading this sort of thing, Todd," she said with concern. "I'm afraid it's going to give you nightmares."

His dad came to his rescue. "It's only make-believe," he assured her. "I used to read this stuff when I was a kid. It's fun."

"Yeah, Mom," Todd agreed. "It's just for fun. I really don't believe any of it." Still, after his parents turned off the lights and closed the door, Todd pulled the covers up to his chin. He scanned the room, trying to see into all of its dark places. Slowly, he drifted off to sleep.

In his dream, Todd had just hit a home run and was sliding into home plate when he sensed something strange along the back of his leg. The feeling was odd enough to tug him from sleep back to reality. He wriggled his legs, but the sensation did not stop. Something rough was lightly scraping the back of his knee. Now wide awake, Todd opened his eyes. He was facing the wall, but he could easily make out the shadow of something leaning over his bed. Turning ever so slightly, he caught a glimpse of the figure. It wasn't very large, but it was powerfully built and covered with thick, dark hair. One furry hand rested lightly on the edge of the bed, and he saw its long claws glinting in the moonlight. To his horror, Todd realized that whatever the thing was, it was licking the back of his leg with its sandpaperlike tongue.

Gathering all of his courage, the boy suddenly yanked his leg away and rolled off the opposite side of his bed. The creature raised itself and uttered a chilling cry. He could see its bloodred eyes grow large. The beast began to edge toward the door. "It's trying to cut me off," Todd realized in panic. "I've got to stop it." He picked up his bedside lamp and hurled it at the creature, screaming "Mom! Dad!" The beast howled and lashed out at him with razor-sharp claws. Todd managed to sidestep the blow as he leapt onto the bed, the beast circling behind him. His path to the door was clear now, but when he tried to jump from the bed, his feet became tangled in the sheets. Todd tumbled to the floor, hitting his head so hard that it made him dizzy. The creature howled. Todd could see saliva dripping from its daggerlike fangs. The terrified boy scrambled to his feet and managed to make it to the hallway and stagger toward his parents' room. He found their door standing open. In the moonlight from the single open window, Todd could distinguish two large, still figures in bed, unmoving in bloodstained sheets. He barely noted that there was only one window on the far wall where he thought there should be two.

Stunned, Todd leaned against the doorway. "Oh, no," he groaned. "This can't be happening." As if in answer, he heard the shuffling sound of the beast as it moved toward him in the darkened hall. It was snuffling and slavering at the mouth. Todd backed slowly into his parents' room. It looked different somehow—not quite as it should be. For a moment, the creature paused in the doorway and looked at the lifeless figures in the bed as if it, too, recognized them. Moaning lightly, it took an uncertain step toward the bed, then it raised its lip in a terrible grimace and advanced toward Todd. Horrified, the boy stepped back as far as he could. He found himself pressed up against a dresser—one he couldn't recall being there before. His hands slid across the polished top until he felt something familiar. It was a large sewing basket. A pair of sharp scissors rested beside it, just out of reach. Todd slowly stretched his fingers toward the scissors while keeping his eyes on the beast's crimson pupils . . . almost . . . almost. Suddenly, the creature lunged, knifelike claws extended toward Todd's throat. The boy felt a sharp pain, then something

warm and wet began to drip down his neck. In a final effort he gripped the scissors and stabbed at the monster with all his might, making a deep slice across one of its outstretched paws.

The beast roared in anguish, cradling its hand and crying. Within seconds, the room's lights came on, revealing the small, furry creature sitting up in bed. Posters of snarling humans stared down from the walls, and books of scary human stories were lined up on the bedside shelf.

The beast's worried parents swept into the room. Its mother gently soothed her frightened child. "Was it another bad dream, dear?" She picked up a magazine that

had slipped to the floor beside the bed. A picture of a human with its teeth bared and a pair of needle-sharp scissors in its hand threatened from the cover. The title identified the story as "Todd the Terror." She looked accusingly at the large male beast at her side. "I told you he shouldn't read that nonsense before bedtime." Then she turned back to her whimpering little monster and started to tuck it back in.

"There, there, dear. Don't cry. You're all right now. There are no such things as humans. They're only make-believe."

What's the Matter with Marvin?

obbie tossed uncomfortably in his bed and drifted toward wakefulness. It was so hot, unbearably hot. Kicking the blankets off his legs, he rolled onto his side, took a deep breath and began to choke uncontrollably. The room was lit with a flickering, eerie, orange glow. The air scalded his throat, and smoke stung his eyes.

"Mom, Dad!" he cried, beating at the red-orange flames licking at the edges of his bedsheets. "Mom!" he screamed and sat upright.

Wide-eyed, Robbie looked around his cool, darkened bedroom. The flames had vanished, but sweat trickled down his neck and soaked the T-shirt that he wore when he slept.

Robbie had been only six when his parents were killed in a fire that had destroyed their home, a fire that he alone survived. His dream brought back jumbled images of that horrible night. Unlike his nightmare, Robbie had seen no flames that night, just billows of black, choking smoke. He had felt his way slowly and painfully out of his bedroom, along the hall, and down the staircase. Blinded by fumes and tears, he had tried to open the front door, but it was stuck. In a panic, Robbie had used a lamp to shatter a window and crawl from the burning house. That had probably been the cause of the short, deep scar he now carried on the left side of his chest. He didn't really know. All he knew for certain was that he was the only one who had escaped.

Robbie ran his fingers over the raised scar. He could hardly remember his parents. The fire had erased everything that might remind him: pictures, cards, the baseball scrapbook he and his dad had put together. After the tragedy, he lived with his grandparents for four years. But recently they had decided that he needed to be around kids his own age. They sent him to live with his uncle Lester and cousin Marvin, whom he had met for the first time earlier that day.

As he sat up in his bed, he listened to the unfamiliar night sounds of his new home. Outside, a cricket sang in the moonlight, and somewhere down below a board creaked as the old house settled. And there was something else. A very soft, whining sound was coming from just down the hall, from Marvin's room. Then it abruptly stopped.

Robbie leaned back and thought about his day as he waited for sleep to return. Uncle Lester had been really nice.

He and Marvin had met Robbie at the train and had taken him to the local diner for the biggest, gooiest hot fudge sundae in the world. Uncle Lester had watched him eat every bite and seemed to be very pleased. Marvin didn't say much and only had a soft drink. It gave him hiccups, which appeared to worry Uncle Lester a lot . . . an awful lot.

Robbie felt his eyelids growing heavy. Maybe Marvin was just nervous about all the changes. Robbie could certainly understand that. Tomorrow would be his first day at Bridgeport Elementary School. As strange as his cousin was, Robbie was glad that Marvin would be with him. He drifted off to sleep with the slightest smell of phantom smoke still in his nostrils.

The next morning, Robbie was very excited as he dressed and hurried downstairs for breakfast. Uncle Lester had prepared toast and scrambled eggs for him, and poured a large glass of freshly squeezed orange juice. Robbie slid into his chair and smiled.

"Good morning, Uncle Lester. This looks great. Thanks."

"Well, you can't get through your first day at school on an empty stomach." Lester smiled and pointed to a brown paper sack on the kitchen counter. "I've made your lunch, too. Don't forget it when you go."

Robbie began to munch a buttery triangle of toast and looked at the sack. "Thanks."

The older man held out a small jar of jam toward his nephew. "Here, why don't you try some of this on your toast? It's strawberry."

"No, thanks. I don't really like strawberry."

Lester's eyebrows raised slightly in surprise. He looked

at the jar in his hand. "You don't like it?"

"No. I'm sorry."

For a moment Lester peered right into Robbie's eyes, then placed the jar on the table. "I thought for sure that I—well, never mind."

At the sound of footsteps in the hall, Robbie turned to see Marvin step into the kitchen. "Hey, Marvin, you'd better sit down and have some breakfast before I finish it all."

Marvin glanced at the table, then to the brown bag on the counter. "I'm not hungry," he replied. "I'm leaving now." He opened the screen door and started down the steps, letting the door slam behind him.

Robbie gobbled down a last bite of toast and drained his glass of juice. Quickly, he gathered up his notebook and lunch bag. "Wait up, Marvin," he called, then looked over his shoulder and added, "Thanks, Uncle Lester. See you later."

Lester stood and moved to the screen door. He waited for several moments watching the two boys, then turned and began to clear the table. He picked up the jam jar and held it in his hand, studying it carefully. "So he doesn't like strawberry."

A little out of breath, Robbie caught up with Marvin at the bus stop. "Hey, what's the hurry?"

Marvin squinted at him as if he were trying to sort something out in his mind. But when the bus pulled up, he boarded without a word, sat in the nearest seat and opened a book. Robbie sat beside his cousin, and they rode to school in silence. At noon Robbie found Marvin alone on a playground bench.

"Hi, Marv. Did you forget your lunch?"

"My name is Marvin."

Robbie sat on the bench. "OK, I'm sorry. Marvin, did you forget your lunch? You can share mine."

"I don't eat lunch," Marvin snapped and walked away. For a moment Robbie stared after him, then he felt a hand on his shoulder.

"Don't worry. He's always like that." Robbie looked up and recognized the boy as one of his new classmates. "I'm Bill. And I'd be happy to share your lunch. What have you got?" The two boys checked out the contents of the paper bag and were soon chattering like lifelong friends. In the shadows of a nearby corridor, Marvin gazed at them stone-faced.

•••••••••

After school, Marvin went straight to his room. Uncle Lester helped Robbie with his homework, then they worked on a jigsaw puzzle together. Robbie became totally absorbed and managed to put the pieces into place one after another. He had the entire picture completed when he realized that Uncle Lester was sitting back, observing him and checking the time on a small stopwatch.

"Whew!" Lester whistled softly. "That's the best time yet."

Robbie opened his mouth to ask what he meant, then paused. Marvin was standing at the edge of the table. With one hand, he swept the puzzle to the floor and glared at Lester. "Was that fast enough? Or maybe it could use a few further adjustments."

"Marvin!" Uncle Lester sounded very angry. "Go to your room."

"What if I don't want to? What if I just stay right here, and we all have a nice little talk. Like about family. How about it, cousin? Don't you want to know all about our family? I'd like to tell you, but you see, I can't. I mean I *really* can't. If I try, I'll just shut down again." Fists clenched, he turned to gaze bitterly at Lester. "You should tell him, you know. He shouldn't have to find out like I did . . . when things start going wrong. But then, this couldn't happen to him. Could it?" Marvin glared hatefully at Robbie. "He's too perfect."

Lester raised himself out of his chair. His voice was curiously deep. "Marvin, go to your room, now!"

The boy stood defiantly for a moment, then spun around and marched out of the room. Without a word, Uncle Lester followed. A moment later came the sound of a door closing upstairs.

Picking up puzzle pieces from the floor, Robbie thought, *There is something really weird going on here.* What was it that Marvin wanted to tell him? What did he mean by "shut down"? Was he sick? Was he just jealous? Robbie crossed to the fireplace to warm his hands. He looked at the collection of photographs framed on the mantelpiece, then realized that something wasn't quite right. All the pictures of Marvin and Lester seemed to be recent, and there wasn't a single picture of Marvin's mom. She had died a year ago in a car accident just before Uncle Lester moved to Bridgeport. Maybe it was still too difficult for them to see a reminder of her. Maybe that was why there were no photographs. But there were no pictures of Marvin as he was growing up either. Robbie made up his mind. Later, after Uncle Lester was asleep, he was going to talk to Marvin. He was going to find out once and for all what was going on.

• • • • • • • • • •

That night Robbie tried to stay awake until he was sure that Lester had gone to bed, but sleep crept up on him, and his dream returned. In it he was lying on the front lawn of his home. He felt the terrible heat from the fire as it consumed everything in its path. He heard the shriek of a siren coming closer and closer. All at once, wide awake, Robbie sat straight up in bed. The sound stopped, but he had heard it. It wasn't a part of his dream. It was a whining noise like the squeal of metal against metal. He strained to listen. Was that something being dragged across the floor? Where was the sound coming from? He slipped out of bed and tiptoed softly into the hall. Now a light tapping noise echoed down the corridor. It was coming from Marvin's room. Robbie crept closer and reached for the doorknob. He turned it slightly, enough to know that it was locked. Staring at the door, Robbie stepped back, and his bare foot landed right on something small, warm and soft. The something squealed and raced down the hall. Robbie jumped, lost his balance and fell against the door. The intruder had only been a frightened mouse. Once the commotion was over, there was no longer any sound coming at all from Marvin's room. Whatever was going on had stopped. He listened at the door, then whispered, "Marvin? Can I come in?" Silence. "Marvin, are you OK? I want to talk to you." Only silence.

•••••••••

The next day was Saturday. Robbie was surprised when Uncle Lester explained that Marvin had gone to visit a friend in nearby Riverside and would be away for the entire weekend. He claimed that he had driven Marvin over himself, earlier that morning. Robbie wasn't convinced, but he didn't ask any questions. Instead, he planned to find the answers himself.

That night after dinner, Lester wanted to work on a new puzzle.

"No thanks, Uncle Lester. I kind of have a stomachache." Robbie watched Uncle Lester's eyes widen, then narrow in disbelief. "I thought I might just go to bed a little early."

"All right," Lester scowled. For a moment he seemed annoyed, then a different expression came over his face, one that frightened Robbie. It was as if he had suddenly made up his mind about something. "I suppose it wouldn't hurt both of us to get some extra rest."

Once upstairs, Robbie waited in his bed. High above, a full moon sailed across the night sky. It bathed the room in ghostly light, while dark shadows crouched in the corners and resisted its glow. Once the house was silent, Robbie crawled out of bed and crept soundlessly to the stairs, edging down them carefully one at a time. The bottom step creaked slightly under his weight. He paused, then continued on until he reached the door to Lester's study. It was ajar and he slipped in. On the wall above his uncle's desk was a board with several hooks. Single, labeled keys hung from each hook.

In the moonlight Robbie could easily read the tags: front door, shed, pickup, basement; the last two keys were not labeled. He lifted them both from their hooks and headed for the stairs. He carefully avoided the squeaky bottom step and was soon standing in front of Marvin's room. He tried the door, but it was locked. Robbie slid the first of the two keys into the lock. It turned and, with a sharp click, the door opened.

The room was dreadfully dark and smelled of oil and ash. Robbie had to grope along the wall as he moved inside. He wasn't really sure what he was looking for, but he knew that something was very wrong, and this room held the clue to what that was. Strangely, there was no furniture in his way. Instead there seemed to be some sort of metal tools hanging from hooks on the wall. When he reached the window, he realized why the room was so dark. Thick boards had been nailed up to keep out the light. His fingers touched a piece of rag that had been jammed in between two boards, and he tugged at it. The rag slipped out, and a sliver of moonlight spilled across the floor. In its dull glow he could see a table in the center of the room. There was something on it. He walked over and reached out to touch the object. It fell to the ground with a thump and rolled into the ribbon of moonlight. Robbie felt a scream well up in his throat. It was Marvin's head!

Suddenly, the room was filled with light. Robbie backed

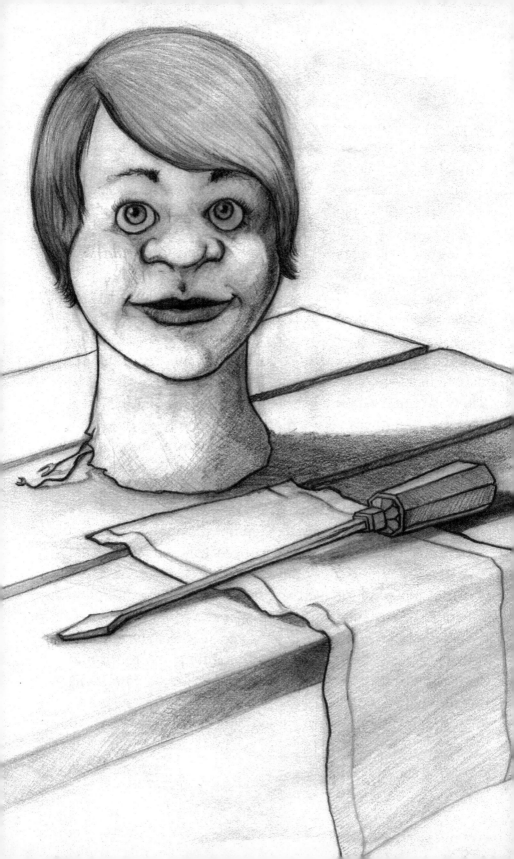

up against the wall when he saw Uncle Lester standing in the open doorway with a broad, flat tool in his hand.

"I'm really sorry you saw this, boy," Lester growled. "I didn't count on you being so curious. That can be a good thing but only in moderation. You're supposed to do everything in moderation. Sneaking around the house at night . . . that's not a good sign. But what's worse is how you lied to me. That's very bad. You didn't have a stomachache tonight."

As Lester moved toward him, Robbie edged away. With a slight bump, his shoulder touched something cool and smooth. Hesitantly, he turned and recognized Marvin's headless form propped up against the wall. Electrical wires stood out from the neck like tentacles. He peeked down at the head in the center of the room. Its sightless eyes stared at the ceiling. Wires snaked from its neck.

Lester pressed closer. "Yes. Marvin is a robot. When I first made him, he seemed so perfect. I thought of everything. I invented a history for him so that the neighbors wouldn't be curious about where his mother was, then I programmed it into his memory. No one suspected, not even Marvin—until that day that he tripped on the stairs and fell. After that, he never could eat or sleep right. I tried to fix the problem, but it just got worse. When his memory failed and he discovered the truth—well, he was only a prototype. I had always planned to just quietly replace him with a much better model. No one would be the wiser. But now you know far too much." Lester raised the bizarre tool in his hand.

Robbie looked around for a way out. "Look, Uncle

Lester, I won't say a thing to anyone. I just want to go back to Grandma and Grandpa's."

"That's quite impossible, Robbie. You see, you never lived there. I had to provide a suitable background for you, too, so the neighbors wouldn't suspect anything when you 'came to live' with us."

"What are you talking about?" Robbie searched frantically for an escape route. "I lived with my grandma and grandpa. They took me in after the fire."

Lester smiled and moved closer. "Yes, the fire. The one that supposedly destroyed all evidence of your parents. Clever little touch, wasn't it? But it was all just a part of your program. Don't worry, with a few minor adjustments and the removal of recent memories, you'll be perfectly all right. You see, Marvin couldn't be repaired." He gripped Robbie by one shoulder and maneuvered the tool to the chest scar. The tool slipped in easily. Robbie felt a strange release of pressure. "But then, he wasn't my greatest achievement." Robbie gaped down at the blinking lights in the now-open compartment in his chest. "You are."

Crying Wolf

 know you don't believe me, but I'm certain it's true!" Anne turned her lower lip down in a pout.

"C'mon, Anne. Think about it," Byron soothed. "It just isn't possible that the zookeepers are really animals in human form. It doesn't make sense."

Byron and Anne were very close friends. They had grown up next door to each other, and he was used to her quirky imagination. Not only did she believe strongly in ghosts, vampires and werewolves, she often made up sinister explanations for the most innocent events. Since a class trip to the zoo last week, Anne had decided that the zookeepers were really animals that had taken temporary human form. She claimed that the beasts planned to lure unsuspecting youngsters into their lair and then devour them. "What makes you so sure they aren't?" Anne demanded for the third time.

"Anne," Byron tried again. "Didn't everybody come back from the zoo? Is anyone missing?"

She simply waved her hand and insisted, "We were just lucky—this time."

Byron shook his head as he watched his friend walk away.

"What kind of story did she cook up this time?" Jon had crept up, and now he playfully punched Byron in the arm. "Does she still think the night janitor is a vampire?" He curled his fingers into imitation claws and bared his teeth.

"No, and don't make fun. She's going to be a great writer someday, and you'll be proud that you knew her."

Jon laughed, but Byron was serious. One of the things that he and Anne shared was a love of science-fiction and horror stories. When they were little, they would spend hours reading sci-fi and scary books and magazines. Eventually, Anne began to make up her own stories. She had notebooks full of them, and Byron loved reading each and every one. She had even worked up the courage to send her favorite story to *Horror Tales* magazine.

Byron shrugged. "It's just that sometimes she lets her imagination get the best of her."

Jon raised his eyebrows. "Right. She's a regular Edgar Anne Poe!"

• • • • • • • • •

After dinner that evening, Byron gathered up his books and went next door. He and Anne usually did their homework together. At a table in the brightly lit kitchen, they were reviewing a list of the state capitals when Anne suddenly looked over her shoulder.

"Did you see that?" she asked.

Byron looked around. "See what?"

"It was something. I just saw it out of the corner of my eye. It moved."

"No, there's nothing."

"I saw something," she insisted.

"And when you looked, it wasn't there."

"Yes."

Byron nodded. "Yeah, I know. Everybody does that sometimes. It's just an optical illusion or something."

They returned to their studies, but Byron noticed that Anne kept shifting her gaze from side to side. Uh, oh, he thought. Now what is she going to come up with?

•••••••••••

It didn't take long for him to find out. The next morning on the bus she was a little jumpy. "You look tired," he remarked as he slid into the seat next to her.

"I am. I didn't get a lot of sleep last night. Do you remember when I told you I thought I saw something out of the corner of my eye? Well, it happened again after you left."

"Anne, I told you that everybody sees that. It's nothing to worry about."

"No, listen," she gripped his arm. "There really was something there. It was a small, dark shape, like a little creature—a gremlin maybe."

"You mean you saw a cute, little, fuzzy, pointy-eared beastie?" Byron teased. "Oh, no. We're all in terrible danger!"

Anne twisted away and looked out the window. "You don't believe me."

• • • • • • • • • •

At lunchtime Byron and his friends always ate in the shade of the largest tree on the playground. He barely had a chance to open his lunch box before Jon started poking around.

"Is that ham and cheese?" Jon craned his neck to see the sandwich that Byron was unwrapping. "If it is, I'll give you my tuna fish."

"No, thanks."

"I'll throw in a bag of potato chips."

Anne pulled her lunch from a brown bag. "If you want peanut butter and jelly, I'll trade with you, Jon."

"How do I know it's peanut butter and jelly and not crunchy werewolf tongues and bat's blood?" Jon put his hands to his throat, crossed his eyes and did an imitation of choking. The other kids giggled, and Anne looked embarrassed. Byron was quick to come to her aid.

"Anything would be better than that cat food you eat every day, Jon." He winked at Anne.

Jon looked sheepish. "You're right. I can't face another

74

day of tuna fish! I was only joking. Peanut butter sounds great." Anne smiled good-naturedly, and they exchanged sandwiches. Jon eagerly unwrapped his prize.

"What! Are you kidding? Somebody's already been eating this." He held out the sandwich to show the tiny bites that had been taken all the way around it.

• • • • • • • • • •

"It must have been a mouse or something," Byron ventured on the bus ride home.

"A mouse," Anne pointed out, "would not rewrap the sandwich after it had taken a few bites. It was *them*. I know who they are. I wrote a story about creatures just like them a while ago—hungry little beasts from a sort of parallel dimension." She paused as if a thought had suddenly occurred to her. "That must be it," she said softly. Anne seemed to be talking more to herself than to her friend. "I know who they are, and now they have to get rid of me. They're all around, just waiting until the right time—when I'm alone."

"Are you still talking about your gremlins? I told you, it's just an optical illusion," Byron said.

"But what if it isn't? What if they are really there, preying on humans as they please, perhaps as food . . . picking us off one by one. People disappear every day!"

Byron felt the hair rise on the back of his neck. Now she was giving him the creeps. "Anne, if that's true, why can't I see them?"

"Because you don't believe they are there. You won't let yourself see them. But I did . . . and now it's too late. I know their secret. I'm a threat to them, and they have to get rid of me."

"You're letting your imagination get the better of you."

"Am I? Is this my imagination?" She held out the book report that she had been working on the night before. A faint trail of very small, humanlike footprints ran along the side of the page.

· · · · · · · · · ·

The next day, Anne showed Byron a large bruise and a scratch on her leg and claimed that *they* were getting bolder.

"I'm really frightened, Byron. They are after me now. I'm afraid that one night they'll come for me, and I'll just disappear."

"Have you talked to your parents?"

"Yes, but they think I'm making it all up," Anne said, almost in tears. "You believe me, don't you? You believe that they're really real?"

Byron wasn't sure what to say. He wanted to help his friend. Finally, he whispered, "Yes, I believe you." For a split second he thought he caught a glimpse of movement nearby.

Byron couldn't sleep that night. He was too worried about Anne. Although it was almost midnight, he could see from his window that the light in her room was still on. At last, he pulled on his clothes, quietly opened his bedroom window and climbed out into the yard. He crept up to

Anne's window. He intended to tap on the glass and ask her to come out, but he never got the chance. As he leaned toward the window, he saw the lamp beside her bed crash to the floor in an explosion of glass. When it fell, he thought he saw Anne crouched at the foot of her bed as if she were trying to hide. Her face was twisted in terror. And something else, too: two or three small figures, half-human and half-beast, loping toward her on long, thin legs, their clawed hands extended . . . maybe . . . but there just wasn't enough time, not enough light. A chill ran down his spine. Had one of the little beings actually turned and looked directly at him with glittering, catlike eyes? He couldn't be sure.

Suddenly, the overhead light blazed. Anne's father entered the room. Her mother stood near the door with her hand on the light switch. Byron crouched down. He watched them scan the bedroom and pick up the broken lamp. He heard them call Anne's name, but she was nowhere to be found.

Byron didn't know what to do. He quickly crossed the distance between the two houses and slipped into his bedroom window. As he was changing back into his pajamas, the telephone rang. He stepped into the darkened hall and saw his mother through the open door of the family room. She was speaking into the receiver.

"No, Angela. Byron is already in bed. She certainly isn't here." She paused as if listening. "I'll talk to him. Then we'll be right over."

Byron couldn't decide what to do. He wasn't really sure what had happened in his friend's now-empty bedroom. He

quickly slipped back to his room and into bed. He could hear his parents' worried voices in the other room. A moment later a sliver of brightness shone under his bedroom door. There was a knock, and his mother opened the door. His father stood behind her. Light from the hall spilled into the room and pooled at the foot of Byron's bed.

"I'm sorry to wake you, dear, but Mrs. Yates just called. She said that Anne is gone. All of her things are there, but she is missing. Did she say anything to you tonight? Was she upset? Do you have any idea where she might be?"

Byron sat up. What could he say? How could he convince them? He knew it sounded crazy, but he said, "Yes,

I think she's in trouble. She told me that there were these things, like gremlins, that were after her. . . . "

"I don't want to hear that kind of nonsense," Byron's father warned. "We all know about her wild imagination. But this is serious."

He looked at his parents. They would never believe it. He wasn't even sure that he did, but he had to do something. He threw the covers back and jumped out of bed.

"It's not just her imagination. You've got to do something," Byron pleaded. "I looked in her window, and I saw them myself! Or at least, I think I did." His parents glanced at each other. "They were small, and they had claws and sharp teeth. I think they took her away. Maybe they killed her! Don't you believe me?" He looked from one to the other. "You *don't* believe me."

Byron's father put his arm around his son's shoulder. "How can we?" he reasoned. "I know this upsets you, but you can't start making up monsters to solve real problems. This is no time for such things. Anne might have run away. She could be in danger. Now, did she say anything to you that might help?"

Byron felt himself go limp. Anne had been really upset. Maybe she really did run away. Maybe he had dreamed the whole thing. "No, Dad. She didn't say anything to me."

"All right. We're going next door to see if we can help."

"Is there anything I can do?"

His mother reached out and stroked his hair. "Not now. Just go back to bed. We'll talk about it in the morning."

Byron looked out across the garden and saw his parents entering the house next door. But what if it wasn't a dream? What if Anne had been right? He glanced down, and his gaze fell on something on the sill of his open window. It was a tiny footprint of some sort . . . something that he had seen once before. Then, just out of the corner of his eye, a slight movement caught his attention, but he turned to find nothing there.

No Laughing Matter

Everyone has something that they are really good at. Gordy Davis was probably best at being just plain mean. He was bigger than the other kids in his class, and he always came out the winner in a fight. But that wasn't good enough for Gordy. He and his four closest friends, Pat, Larry, Jasper and Roy, spent hours figuring out practical jokes that would make other people miserable. The more mean-spirited the prank, the better they liked it. They had formed a club called the Jokers, and each of the boys wore a cap adorned with that name.

Most of the other kids in class tried to stay out of their way and were careful not to annoy them. No one ever told an adult about the spiteful things the boys did. Some actually did favors for the Jokers, hoping to stay on their good side. Mitch Harrigan did Gordy's math homework every day. Even that didn't always save Mitch, though. The week before, Mitch had gotten several answers wrong, and Gordy received a C minus. On Friday Mitch found his bicycle wedged among the low branches of a tree. The Jokers stood around and had a good laugh while he tried to get it down. At first no one would risk helping him, but when the bike started to fall, the new kid in town, Rick Porter, raced forward and steadied it. He then helped Mitch lift it to the ground while Gordy glared.

Rick and his parents had moved to town during the summer, and this was his first year at Washington Elementary. It hadn't taken him long to make friends. He was easygoing and fun to be with. He was also one of the few kids who didn't back down from the Jokers. For a while Gordy had avoided Rick. Now, he would have to be dealt with, too.

· · · · · · · · · ·

Monday morning, Gordy joined his buddies on the playground before class began.

"Did you get it?" he whispered to Roy.

"Yeah." The boy proudly held up a small brown paper bag. He turned his head from side to side to be sure that no one was watching, then reached into the bag and pulled out a large glass jar. It was half-filled with squirming mealworms.

Jasper made an ugly face. "Yuck! They're really disgusting!"

"Perfect!" Gordy smirked. "This should teach that little creep to mind his own business. And if it doesn't, I've got something else in mind. Now remember," he said as he put a hand on Larry's shoulder, "you wait until everyone else puts their things away on the shelf, then you go back like you're gonna put your stuff away, too."

"I know." Larry shifted uneasily. "And while nobody's looking I dump the creepy crawlers into Rick's lunch box. What if I get caught? How come I have to do it?"

Gordy tightened his hold on the boy's shoulder. "Because I said so. Besides, your section on the shelf is right next to Rick's. Nobody will notice what you're doing. I'll see to that. Now let's go."

The boys joined the group of children waiting in the school hall. Once Mrs. Jandrew unlocked and opened the door, they all filed in. Chattering and laughing, the kids walked to the back of the room. Lining the back wall was a tall set of wooden shelves divided into sections. Each section had a student's name written above it on a paper label. The cubicles were used to store coats, extra books, lunch boxes or anything else not needed during class. Larry watched as Rick stuffed his baseball jacket in the space under his name and then set his lunch box down. Once everyone was sitting down, Larry stood nervously and picked up his sweater and the paper sack Roy had given him. He sauntered to the shelf and, with his back to the room, slipped out the glass jar and unscrewed the lid. At that moment Gordy jumped up, pointed under the teacher's desk, and yelled.

"Mrs. Jandrew! A mouse!"

Several of the kids squealed, and Mrs. Jandrew hastily pushed back her chair. During the commotion, Larry opened the lid of Rick's lunch box, tipped in the worms, and snapped the box shut. He was back in his seat by the time the teacher announced that there was nothing under her desk.

"I guess I was mistaken," Gordy grinned. As he sat down, he turned to look at his accomplice. Larry nodded slightly.

• • • • • • • • • •

At lunchtime the Jokers could hardly control their laughter as they watched Rick settle at a table with several friends. Rick had purchased a container of fruit punch and opened it while he listened to one of the group explain the gory details of a movie he had seen over the weekend. It was about a town that had been attacked by thousands of deadly snakes. As he described a scene in which the hero woke up and found his bed covered with slithering reptiles, Rick, without looking, popped open his lunch box and reached inside.

"*Aaaaaaaahhhhhhhh!*" he howled. Spilling the entire carton of punch down the front of his shirt, Rick yanked his hand away as if he had been bitten. The lunch box tipped onto its side and several dozen wriggling mealworms rolled out. Everyone at the table shrieked. The boy who had been telling the story jumped up so quickly that his chair tipped over and clattered to the floor. The uproar spread to the kids seated nearby. They squealed and backed away, scraping their chairs across the floor in alarm or tipping them over, adding to the chaos.

Gordy couldn't hold back. He laughed so hard that he doubled over in his chair. When things quieted down, he sat up to see Rick standing over him.

"You did that. Didn't you?" the enraged boy demanded.

Gordy smirked, "What's the matter? Can't take a joke?"

"It wasn't funny!" Rick was so angry he was almost in tears. His hands were bunched into fists. "It was stupid. Like you!"

Gordy rose slowly. He towered over the other boy. "Take that back."

"I'm not afraid of you or anything else."

Gordy's mouth twisted into a crooked scowl, then slowly a different expression washed over his face.

"OK," he said smiling. "Prove it."

"What?"

"You're right. That was a mean thing to do. But I'll tell you what. If you can prove that you really aren't afraid of anything, if you accept my challenge, then I'll apologize, and I'll never pick on you again. We could even be friends."

Gordy's pals exchanged surprised glances.

"I don't want to be your friend," Rick growled. "But you would apologize in front of everyone?"

"Yes."

"And you wouldn't bother me again?"

"Guaranteed."

"What sort of challenge?"

Gordy lowered his voice conspiratorially, "Have you ever heard of the Banwell place?"

Rick nodded. Everyone knew about that old house. It was one of the first things he had learned from the other kids when he came to town. Most people avoided even walking past it if they could. No one was certain who had been the original owner, but old Mr. Banwell was supposed to have lived in it for at least thirty years. He had been pretty eccentric and had even fancied himself a warlock or something. People said that on some nights they could see weird lights moving through the halls and hear strange noises. Nobody really knew how the old man had died, either. One day about ten years ago, the postman just found Banwell face down out in his front yard. When he rolled Banwell over, the expression frozen on the dead man's face had been one of unearthly terror.

"Well," Gordy went on, "all you have to do is spend one hour in there, starting at midnight."

Rick's jaw dropped. "Alone? My parents would never let me do that."

"Don't worry. I'll have a sleep-over at my house this weekend. My parents won't even notice if we sneak out. It'll be over before you know it—if you really are brave enough. Deal?" He extended his hand.

Rick reached out and took it. "Deal."

•••••••••

After school, Gordy and his cohorts walked home. At first they were silent, then Pat spoke up.

"Are you really gonna apologize to that little jerk in front of everybody?"

"Nah," Gordy said, shaking his head. "He'll never make it through an hour in that house."

"But what if he does?" Jasper complained.

"He won't. We're going to fix it so that he won't stay in there more than a few minutes. I've got it all figured out." The glimmer of evil in Gordy's eyes made the other boys shudder.

• • • • • • • • • •

Over the next few days, the gang worked on props for the weekend. On Saturday morning the boys slipped into the Banwell house through a side window to set everything up.

"I don't like it here," Larry whined. "I don't know if this is such a good idea."

Roy was making a sizable stain on the wall with fake blood. "It's a great idea! If this place is so creepy during the day, imagine how bad it will be at night. Particularly when we're finished with it." He winked at Jasper, who had just taken a large dead rat from a shoe box.

"Where should I put this?" Jasper asked, holding the rat by the tail as far away from himself as he could.

Gordy looked around. "Put it near the window. When the trick flashlight goes out, he'll probably try to open the curtains to get more light."

Pat shuddered. "He might step on it. Gross!"

"Yeah, but this will be the best gag of all." Gordy slipped a tape into a complicated-looking player that he had hidden in a closet next to the staircase. He stood back and pushed a button on a small remote control that he held in his hand. At first there was a soft, eerie shuffling noise. Next came the sound of ragged breathing that seemed to be coming closer and closer.

"That's great!" Roy giggled. Suddenly a horrible moan issued from the tape player and filled the room. "That's enough for me! I'm getting out of here!"

Laughing and horsing around, they ran most of the way to Gordy's house.

· · · · · · · · · ·

That night Rick's parents dropped him off at Gordy's house. The boys spent the evening watching a scary movie and telling ghost stories. As midnight approached, Gordy began a tale about the Banwell house.

"Folks say that old Mr. Banwell used to try to conjure up spirits and stuff. After he died, his daughter took over the house. She was some sort of professor or something and didn't believe the things that people were saying . . . like about the lights and the noises. Everything seemed to be all right at first. But then, on the first night of the new moon, something happened. It was a night kind of like tonight. The Hansens, who live down the hill from the old place, said that it was shortly after midnight when they heard the moaning . . . that horrible moaning. In the morning they found her—Banwell's daughter—wandering in the woods behind the house. Her long, black hair had turned completely white! She kept talking about the thing, begging it to leave her alone. From what she said, the sheriff figured it had one arm and one terrible, glowing eye! And it smelled like . . . well, it was that old musty smell that comes from something that has been buried for a long, long time. The rumor is that a couple of years later they found another body just sitting on the porch. It was a kid who had been missing for a while. At least they thought it was him. You see, it didn't have a head. Of course, that can't be true." Gordy paused for effect. "Or can it?" With an exaggerated shiver, he looked at the clock. "It's time."

One at a time, the boys eased out of the bedroom window. No one spoke as they approached the dark, brooding house. The windows stared down at them like demon eyes as they crept up the walk to the front porch.

"Here. You'll need this." Gordy slipped a flashlight into Rick's hand. "You have to go through that open window," he said as he pointed to the one near the door, the one that the Jokers had used in the morning when they set up the prank. "It's the only way in or out. Everything else is locked or boarded up. We'll stay here to be sure you don't sneak out." He looked at the glowing numbers on his watch. Both hands pointed straight up. "Go."

Rick didn't say anything, but he was trembling. As he crawled over the windowsill, he began to have a change of heart. With a shaking hand, he played the beam of light around the deserted room. He froze as he noticed the brick-red blood splashed against the wall. Forcing his feet to move, Rick edged along the opposite wall. His foot nudged something soft. Just before the flashlight failed, he saw the body of the rat. Outside, Gordy pressed a button. Inside,

there was a soft, muffled scraping noise. Rick backed toward the open window as the sound of ragged breathing seemed to come from everywhere. The moan had only begun when Rick scrambled back out of the window and down the path.

"Nothing is worth staying in there," he gasped. "You can keep your apology and your stupid club!"

"What'd I tell you?" Gordy gloated to the others as he watched Rick disappear down the block.

The boys exchanged high fives. Larry patted Gordy on the back and chuckled.

"I can't wait to tell everyone tomorrow about the look on his face when he came flying through the window. Now can

we get out of here? This place gives me the willies!"

Everybody laughed in agreement, including Gordy.

"Sure we can. Just as soon as we get the tape recorder."

The laughter stopped. "You mean, go in there . . . now?" Pat gawked at Gordy.

"Of course, now. You don't think I'm gonna leave it here!"

Larry started to back away from the others. "I'm not going in there."

"Me neither," Jasper whispered.

Gordy looked from one to the other. "What's the matter with you guys? Roy? C'mon."

Roy shook his head no. "If you're so brave, why don't you go in alone?"

"Well, then I guess I will. What a bunch of chickens!"

Angrily, Gordy ducked into the open window. Once inside, he switched on the flashlight. It sputtered to life, then failed, leaving him in shadow once again. "Stupid thing," he muttered. "It's no better than the one I gave Rick."

Slowly, he eased forward into the room and moved toward the staircase. The boards creaked under his feet. If something was in the house, it would sure know he was here. He brushed the thought aside.

"There's nothing in here," he reassured himself. That was when he heard the slight shuffling sound that seemed to be moving closer. He felt in his pocket. The remote control was gone.

"Right, guys," he said under his breath. "Very funny." The ragged breathing began by the time he reached the closet door. Gripping the handle, he opened it.

"That's funny." He wrinkled his nose when he detected a powerful, musty odor. "I didn't notice that smell this morning."

He knelt down to pick up his tape recorder. As he heard the low, chilling moan behind him, his brain barely registered that the tape recorder was not running. The taste of fear welled up in Gordy's mouth as he whirled to stare into the single, glowing eye of horror. The foul, putrid stench grew overpowering as the huge, shadowy creature loomed over its crouching victim. Cloaked in rotten rags, its skeletal arm darted out and gripped Gordy's throat in one clawed hand. The thing drew him across the floor, opening its gaping mouth to reveal many rows of serrated teeth.

"I get so few visitors here," it rasped, lifting the terrified boy completely off the ground. "But those who join me never leave. I guess the joke is on you."

Family Ties

O JOB TOO BIG OR TOO SMALL, proclaimed the headline on the colorful fliers Jamie stuffed in mailboxes all over her neighborhood. The jobs listed included lawn mowing, gardening, light housework, baby-sitting and pet walking. At the bottom of the leaflet, Jamie's name and phone number appeared in block letters.

"This is cool," Rachael, Jamie's best friend, remarked as she slipped a flier through a mail slot in her next-door neighbor's door. "You'll make a fortune! How did you get your parents to agree to let you do this?"

"They get to screen everyone who calls." Jamie rolled her eyes. "I guess I understand why they are so cautious.

Today's newspaper has a huge article about another student from the junior college who is missing. That makes three in five months. That's the reason I promised that I would only pass out fliers in our neighborhood."

"Well," Rachael said, shrugging. "I wish I'd thought of it."

It didn't take long for the calls to start. That evening two people called to offer dog-walking jobs. Another called for lawn mowing.

"It looks like your business is off to a good start," her father observed. "You'll have to plan carefully to get everything done. And remember—"

"Homework comes first!" they said together.

"I know, Dad." Jamie grinned. "Don't worry." The phone rang again, and Jamie's mother answered it. She spoke for a while and asked a few questions, then put her hand over the mouthpiece.

"Jamie. It's Mr. Hubbard over on Ravenwood. He wants to talk to you."

Jamie took the receiver from her mom. "Hello?"

"Hello, Jamie. I received your notice this evening, and I believe I could use your assistance."

I'll bet, Jamie thought. In her mind she could picture the timeworn house that Mr. Hubbard had moved into six months ago. It was very large, with an attic and a full basement. There supposedly were secret passageways, too.

"I'd be happy to help, Mr. Hubbard," she said into the phone. "What would you like me to do?"

"Just help me tidy up and care for a few things on a regular basis. You see, I am a historian, and I'm working on a new book. I spend my days doing research, and I teach at the college in the evenings. I'm afraid I don't have time for anything else. If you come over, I could show you around, and we could settle on your fee."

"That sounds fine. I'll be over right after school tomorrow."

"Oh . . . no. I'm afraid that won't work. I won't be home until just after dark."

"All right. Would 6:30 be OK?"

"Yes. That would be perfect. Thank you."

"I've got another one," Jamie beamed as she joined her family at the dinner table.

"I know Mr. Hubbard," her older sister, Jennifer, said. "He just started teaching Eastern European history at the college." She plopped a serving of steaming mashed potatoes on her plate. "He's kind of eccentric."

"In what way, Jen?" her mother asked.

"Well, some of the kids in the class say that he talks about things that happened hundreds of years ago like he'd actually spoken to someone who lived back then."

Her father passed the vegetables to Jamie. "That just sounds like he's a good teacher. You know what I've always told you about jumping to conclusions. Now, how about passing those rolls?"

· · · · · · · · · ·

In the failing light of dusk, the old house did look kind of creepy. As promised, Jamie was standing on the raised wooden porch at exactly 6:30. She rang the doorbell and heard it echo through the large rooms inside. There was no answer. She rang it again and waited. Leaning out over the wooden railing, she tried to peer into the window, then turned her attention back to the door. It was wide open, and Mr. Hubbard was standing there, staring down at her.

"Oh!" she started. "I didn't hear you."

"I'm sorry," he said, smiling. His face seemed uncomfortable with the expression. "I didn't mean to frighten you. Please, come in."

The inside of the house was as old and worn-looking as the outside, but it was filled with what appeared to be valuable antiques. What particularly caught her eye was a beautiful, engraved sword hanging over the fireplace. Its edge was razor sharp, and its hilt looked as if it was made of silver.

"I am mainly concerned with keeping the front room tidy. I don't want my special mementos collecting dust." Raising an eyebrow, he added, "Besides, students visit me on occasion." He handed her a key. "Twice a week should be quite sufficient. I don't mind when you schedule the work. Just be certain to be finished before dusk. I prefer to have the house to myself after that. And one other thing." He pointed to a door at the end of the hall. "That is the basement door. It is always locked because I store my research material down there. Please don't bother with it. I have the only key." He promised to leave her fee in an envelope on the mantelpiece at the beginning of each week.

• • • • • • • • •

At school the next day, Rachael wanted to hear every detail about Mr. Hubbard and the new job. She had already decided that anyone who would live in that house had to be weird.

"I can't believe you really go into that creepy old place!" Rachael wrinkled her nose.

Jamie shook her head. "It's not so bad. Besides, no one will be there to bother me."

"You mean you're going to go in alone?"

"Sure. Why not?"

"Because of all the weird stuff that is going on lately. You know why Tim Wyzok wasn't in school today? His sister disappeared! That makes four people missing. Something very strange is going on."

Jamie remembered Rachael's words as she entered the house on Ravenwood late that afternoon. In spite of her insistence that everything was all right, something about the place really bothered her. It was so quiet, yet she sensed that she was not alone. As the feeling grew stronger, Jamie turned to look over her shoulder as she dusted. Her duster accidentally knocked a small carved box to the floor.

"Oh, no! I hope it isn't broken," she said to herself. Kneeling to pick up the fallen object, she noticed that a word, perhaps a name, was carved in the lid—Trouvese. Then she saw something glittering on the floor, something that must have been in the box. She saw that it was a ring with a large red stone and a distinctive golden "T" inlaid in the center. She was about to slip it onto her finger when a light, scraping noise caught her attention. It was coming from the basement. Something—someone—was plodding up the stairs. Jamie looked at the lengthening shadows around her. It was late! Trembling, she returned the ring to the box, raced out of the door and ran the two blocks to her home.

•••••••••

The next day, Jamie stopped at the public library on her way home from school. Methodically, she scrolled through the computerized card catalog that referred to subjects beginning with "T," searching for the odd name she had seen the evening before.

"Trout, trouveres, Trouvese!" There were two references. She copied the call numbers down on a slip of paper and practically sprinted to the bookshelf. Running her finger along the rows of books, Jamie found the ones she wanted. One was a book about Eastern European nobility. It included a reprint of an aged and cracked portrait of a nobleman, Baron Trouvese. "Wow," she whispered softly. "He looked an awful lot like Mr. Hubbard." Suddenly her eyes grew wide. "His ring. It's just like the one I found yesterday!"

The second reference to Trouvese was in a book about witchcraft and demons. Jamie found the entry she wanted and read it aloud to herself slowly and carefully. "In 1517, a series of disappearances in the village of Pizen caused an outbreak of fear and panic. The blame for the missing children was finally placed on a local noble, Baron Trouvese. He was proclaimed a vampire and put to death by beheading." The portrait shown also looked remarkably like Mr. Hubbard, and the distinctive family ring adorned the

Baron's finger. At the bottom of the page was a drawing of the sword used to execute the accused vampire. It was exactly like the sword that hung over the fireplace of the house on Ravenwood!

Jamie slammed the book shut. "That's why all the disappearances. Baron Trouvese and Mr. Hubbard are the same. He's been preying on the students!" Jamie felt the panic in her rising. "I've got to tell someone, but I'll need proof. I've got to get that ring!" She made copies of the portraits. In the sky the afternoon sun hung above the horizon. It took a few minutes for her to get to the house, but there was still time. She used her key to enter and stood for a moment in the marbled foyer, straining to hear the slightest sound. Slowly, she stole into the parlor. The box was as she had left it on the table. Her heart raced as she reached out her hand and. . . .

"Jamie, what are you doing here today?"

Her notebook clattered to the floor. Jamie whirled around to come face-to-face with Mr. Hubbard. He frowned down at her and reached to the floor to pick up the notebook.

"I know what you are," she gasped.

"Do you? And what is that?"

"You're a vampire!"

He began to laugh. "If that's true, aren't I supposed to be tucked away in a coffin somewhere until sundown?"

Jamie glanced out the window. The sun was just sinking to the horizon, but the landscape still glowed with its failing light. Suddenly, she didn't feel quite so sure of herself. "But . . . the ring . . . and the pictures."

"Ah, yes." He flipped open the box and took out the ring. "It belonged to a distant relative of questionable character. Supposedly, he was beheaded, you know." He smiled evilly. "The poor villagers didn't know that it was important to burn the body afterward. Instead, they let the immediate family take it away."

"Then you . . . you're not . . . ," Jamie searched frantically for an avenue of retreat. She backed into the room, away from Mr. Hubbard.

"Oh, no, my dear girl. I'm as human as you are. It is merely my privilege to be one in a long line of direct family members to care for the Baron's things. You see, the Baron had a brother who did not suffer from the same—shall we call it 'affliction?' It was this devoted brother who claimed the body and continued to care for its 'special needs.' I am directly descended from that brother, so I suppose you might call the Baron my great uncle—many times removed." Mr. Hubbard noticed the copy of the Baron's portrait that had slipped from Jamie's notebook to the floor. "The family resemblance is striking. Don't you think? It is a large family. When I die, there are others from the homeland who can take my place when he needs them."

The last rays of sunlight faded from the window. "You mean, in case he ever comes back from the dead?"

"Not at all." Mr. Hubbard stepped toward the front door and slowly slid the bolt into place. He looked beyond her toward the basement door. "Did I say he was dead?"

A scream caught in Jamie's throat as she turned to see the hideous sneer of the ancient Baron Trouvese, who stood in the doorway of the basement. His face was as pale as moonlight, but his fangs glittered and his eyes glowed bloodred as his gaze locked onto hers. The ghastly night creature stepped slowly forward, a predator that had sighted its helpless victim. Jamie couldn't move. She was trapped. The room filled with the stench of death. The Baron licked his colorless lips with a crimson tongue. Paralyzed with fear, Jamie realized what had happened to the missing students. Clawed hands raised, fangs bared, Baron Trouvese swept toward her.

Nine Lives

Jason was certain there wasn't a computer game around that he couldn't win or another player who could beat his scores. Well, there was one person who could hold his own in a competition. Until a couple of weeks ago, Steve had been Jason's very best friend, but now Steve was avoiding him. In school on Monday Jason decided to find out what was wrong. When he saw Steve turn the corner and approach the front entrance, he trotted up to meet him.

"Hey, buddy," Jason said, trying to sound casual. "I was waiting for you."

Steve flinched and stepped back. He looked startled as

he glanced from side to side, then slowly relaxed.

"What for?" His voice was sullen.

"Well, I got this new game. It's called 'Barbary Coast.' It's got pirates and stuff, and you have to find this treasure before the pirates capture you and make you walk the plank."

Steve looked up. For a moment his expression changed as if he was about to ask something, but he didn't. He fixed his stare on the ground and moved on.

"C'mon, buddy," Jason tried one more time. "You can come over after school. Look, if something is bothering you, I want to help." He put his hand on his friend's shoulder.

Steve shrugged it off. "No. I can't." He halted and peered directly into Jason's eyes. He seemed frightened. "And stay away from me. I mean it."

When Jason's mother knocked on the door of his room the following Saturday and told him that Steve had come to visit, Jason was really surprised. He was even more surprised when he saw that his friend looked as if he hadn't slept in days. Dark circles ringed his eyes. He was pale, and his hands were shaking slightly.

"Look, Jason," Steve began when the two friends were alone in his room. "I know I've been acting weird lately, but . . . maybe I shouldn't ask . . . but I need your help. I think you're the only one who can help me." He ran his fingers through his hair, trying to choose his words carefully. "I'm not sure how to say this. I don't know if you'll believe me."

"Try me." Jason watched as Steve fumbled in his jacket pocket and pulled out a small computer disk. He placed it carefully on the edge of the desk and stepped back as if the thing might make some sort of move on its own.

"Do you remember the store down on Foothill Boulevard that used to sell old comic books and baseball cards and stuff?"

Jason thought for a moment. "Oh, yeah. It closed down last year, didn't it? There was a fire or something."

"Yeah, but a couple of weeks ago I rode by on my bike, and a new store was in its place. It had a display of computer games in the window and a big orange sign that said 'Grand Opening.'"

Jason was interested. "I didn't know a new store had opened. Did it have anything good?"

"That's what was so strange." Steve sank down onto the edge of the bed. "All they had was one game. It was called 'Nine Lives.' The guy in the store was odd, too. When he asked if he could help me, I told him I was just looking and that I didn't have any money. He said that it was no problem, that I could take a copy of the game home with me and try it."

"He let you take it home for nothing?" asked Jason, rather envious.

"Yeah. He said I would come back to give him payment in full. Everyone always came back, he said. I didn't know what he meant then, but I should have just turned around and walked out. Now it's too late. I've started, and I have to keep playing. I tried to take it back, but the store isn't there anymore."

"You mean it went out of business already?"

"No. It's more like it was never even there to begin with. The place is all boarded up, and there are stains on the outside walls from the fire—just like it used to look."

It was easy to see that Steve was serious. Jason picked up the game disk and examined it. It looked like any other. He started to slip it into his computer.

"No. Wait!" Steve gripped him by the wrist. "Once you start it, you can't stop."

"I know what you mean," Jason said, laughing, and slid the disk into the slot in the computer. Immediately, the title of the game appeared on the screen, surrounded by a standard assortment of mythical beasts. A flame-spouting dragon crouched atop the first "N." A two-headed vulture was perched on the "I," and a razor-clawed ogre leaned against the following letter. There were nine creatures in all, one for each letter. A skeleton controlled the "V," and a huge beast with the head of a bull with long curved horns straddled the "E" in LIVES. The last character was an evil-eyed sorcerer standing beside a large box with a small, slender opening at one side and an oval inset of some kind. At the center of the oval was a picture of a bizarre lock. Jason shivered as the image filled the screen.

Steve shook his head and sighed heavily. "The game doesn't stop when the computer is off. Those . . . things," he said, gesturing toward the images of the beasts, "can show up anywhere, anytime. If you don't meet their challenge, you must give up a life. One that is close to you. Once you start to play, you have to continue. The last life at risk is your own. But it isn't just your life that is at stake, it is your soul." Steve reached out and touched the figure of the sorcerer on the computer. "That's what he really wants. By playing the game you enable him to take your soul captive. To save it, you have to find the sorcerer's hiding place and release it. If he destroys you first, then your soul is his forever."

"It sounds cool," Jason replied as he clicked into the game. Several options appeared on the screen.

"You don't understand!" Steve wailed. Jason stopped. "It's for real! I didn't believe it either. But in the past two weeks, too many things have happened. Remember Jojo?" Jason nodded. Jojo the canary had been a birthday present. "The day I lost the first challenge I found him dead at the bottom of his cage. After the next loss, my cat, Jericho, got out of the house and was hit by a car. I knew then that I shouldn't play anymore. But the creatures in the game don't let you stop. They can show up anywhere. And it gets worse . . . my next door neighbor . . . that was my fault."

"Mr. Davis fell from a ladder while he was working on his roof," Jason answered softly. "How could that be your fault?"

"It was no accident." Steve lowered his head into his hands. "And ten days ago my cousin was killed when the brakes on his car failed. And my grandfather—" his voice faltered. "He died last week of a heart attack. The score is 5–0. I don't know who will be next . . . maybe my sister or my parents." The boy looked up at his friend. "You said you wanted to help me. I can't defeat it. I'm not good enough—but together we are. We might have a chance. But if you agree, you'll be in danger. Your soul could be held captive, too."

It all sounded crazy, but Jason realized that Steve believed it was true, and he had to do something to help him. He glanced at the screen. There was an option that read DO YOU WISH TO ADD A PLAYER TO YOUR TEAM? He lightly touched the keyboard. A warning appeared: ARE YOU SURE?

CONSEQUENCES OF LOSS WILL TRANSFER TO NEW PLAYER. Jason looked at Steve, then tapped the key again. A single word appeared: ACCEPTED. A cold chill ran through Jason's body. He felt terribly empty and alone. He barely heard Steve thanking him over and over for joining him.

When Steve left, the strange feeling passed. Jason sat down at the computer and clicked the box that said NEW PLAYER. Of course he didn't accept all of this, but he was curious about the game because it had made his friend so upset. Since he was entering the contest at the point where Steve had left off, the score was already 5–0. In this round he chose a sword as his weapon and battled a winged serpent through a challenging maze. It was close for a first try, but he lost. In the lower corner of the screen, the score flipped to 6-0. Disappointed, he turned off the computer and flopped down on his bed. He tapped at the glass of the small, dry aquarium on the nightstand next to the bed, but his pet iguana didn't move. Slowly, he stood, reached into the aquarium and nudged the animal slightly. It was dead.

That night Jason was awakened by an eerie glow in his room. As he sat up, he noted that the computer was on. The screen read ROUND 7. From somewhere in the room he heard a distant scraping noise that seemed to be drawing nearer. He tipped his head. It seemed to be right . . . (nearer and nearer) . . . under . . . (nearer and nearer) . . . his bed! A bony hand shot out from under the mattress and clamped his ankle in a painful grip. As hard as he struggled, he couldn't break free. It pulled him to the floor and dragged him relentlessly under the bed. Jason clawed at the rug, crumpling it in his hands, but it did no good. He was being drawn under the bed and into a pitch-dark pit. Suddenly, a hand reached out to grasp his. He saw Steve's face. He heard his friend's voice as if from a great distance.

"Hang on! Please! Hang on!"

He clasped Steve's hand with all of his might, but Jason felt his grip weakening inch by inch, until he slipped away. Helpless, he felt himself falling and falling.

• • • • • • • • • •

With a yelp, Jason opened his eyes and sat straight up in bed. Sweat poured down his face as he looked around the room in panic, then he began to relax. "It was only a dream," he decided. But when his gaze fell on the computer screen, in the lower left-hand corner the score read 7–0. At the edge of his bed, he noticed that the rug was crumpled into a knot. Slowly, he pushed back the sheets. Dark bruises were forming on his ankle.

It wasn't a dream. It's just like Steve said, he thought in horror. They can be anywhere. As he tried to make sense of what had happened, Jason became aware of the sound of the telephone ringing. After a few moments he heard crying from downstairs. He slipped out of bed and crept toward the kitchen. Although the clock read 3:20 A.M., the lights were on and he could hear his father's voice.

"Dad?" Jason blinked in the glare of the brightly lit room. His mother was sitting at the kitchen table, sobbing. Beside her, his father sat stroking her shoulder and speaking in low tones. "Dad, what's wrong?"

"Jason," his father motioned to him to come in as his mom sat up and dried her reddened eyes. "It's Uncle Phil." Phil was his mother's younger brother. He had left for vacation only the night before. "He's—there's been an accident."

Jason waited until his parents had gone to bed, then slipped out just after dawn and raced to Steve's house three blocks away.

"Steve," he whispered hoarsely, trying to catch his breath. He tossed pebbles at the window glass of his friend's second-story bedroom. The window slid open, and Steve leaned out. He, too, was fully dressed and wide awake.

"Jason? I'll be right down."

A moment later the boys were standing side by side in the early morning light.

"My uncle," Jason gasped. "I thought it was a dream, but. . . . "

"I know what happened. I saw it on my computer. I tried to help, but I wasn't strong enough to hold you. I'm feeling weaker all the time. What are we going to do? We don't know when or where the next round will take place. I'm sorry I got you into this. If it were just a regular game, it would be easy, but this is different."

Jason tilted his head slightly. "What did you say?"

"This is different from—"

"Maybe it isn't," Jason interrupted. "The key to winning any game is paying attention and staying one step ahead! We know where the next round takes place if we choose it. I say, we go ahead and find the sorcerer now."

"But we have no idea who or where he is."

"Sure we do. You already talked to him."

Steve's eyes lit up. "The man in the store where I got the game!"

"Right! He said you would be back, and you will . . . but before he is expecting you. I have another idea, too. If my hunch is correct, we will need the game disk and probably a flashlight. And there's one other thing I have to do. We can stop at my house on the way."

•••••••••

It was still early when they reached the store on Foothill Boulevard. As Steve had said, it looked as if it had never been opened since the fire. The windows were still boarded up. The boys picked their way to the back entrance. There they pried up a board and managed to crawl inside. Both felt their strength draining with each passing moment. Jason pulled out his flashlight. He played the slender beam around the room.

"It doesn't look like anybody has been in here in a long time."

"I was," Steve whispered, shivering slightly.

"When you first saw the man, where had he come from?"

Steve looked around. "Things are different now, but I think he came in from over there." He pointed to a door just beyond a low archway. The boys moved quickly toward the door. Suddenly, Steve toppled forward, his hands flailing in the air. Jason barely managed to grab his friend's wrist, preventing him from being swallowed up in what appeared to be a dark pit.

"Hang on!" Jason grunted as he yanked Steve back, sending both of them to the ground. Once he had caught his breath, Jason shone the light across the floor. Directly in their path was a gaping hole. Both boys crawled to the cavity and peered over the edge. In the flashlight beam they could see that the pit was about twenty feet deep, and the bottom of it was covered with slithering, writhing snakes!

"Whew!" Steve gasped. "That was close. We must be on the right track. We've got to be careful, though, there might be other traps."

With renewed caution, the boys made their way around the pit to the door and tried the knob.

"It's locked," Jason huffed. He ran his fingers along the edge. "Wait. There's a slot here. Maybe it's like one of those card-key locks." Smiling, he took the game disk from his pocket and slipped it into the slot. The door clicked and opened slowly. Jason removed the disk, and the two boys eased into the room. At the far wall stood what looked like some sort of strange computer, with a blank, oval-shaped screen. It was just like the contraption the sorcerer stood next to in the title drawing.

"This is it," Jason murmured. "This is where he plays the game." They advanced toward the bizarre machine; then with a whine, the oval screen sputtered to life. As in the drawing, the image of a lock was at its center.

"Now what?" Steve was trembling.

Jason stood before the machine. He slipped in the disk and fingered the keyboard. "I'm sure that releasing this lock will free us. I just have to figure out how to . . . DELETE!" The command materialized on the screen, and the lock disappeared. Jason laughed aloud. "That's it." But his smile faded as the lock quickly reappeared. "Wait. What's wrong? What did I miss?"

From the shadows near the open door behind them, a deep voice growled, "You didn't really think it would be that simple, did you?"

Whirling, the boys came face-to-face with the sorcerer himself. He towered above them, his eyes glittering in horrible triumph. "Did you forget the rules? They are quite clear. To release your souls, you must find where they are hidden and then save them." The boys backed away. "It's rather a pity," he whispered ominously as he advanced toward them. "You came so close. Much closer than most." With long, gnarly fingers, the sorcerer reached out and slipped Jason's game disk from the slot in the computer. He held it up for them to see. "Yes, a pity. They were imprinted right in here, under your nose." With a wave of his hand, the disk disappeared. "But it's far too late now."

While he spoke, a luminous mist began to gather in the center of the room. A dark shape took form in the whirling mist. With a blood-chilling snarl, a monstrous beast emerged. It had the body of a man and the head of a bull. Saliva oozed from its gaping mouth, and blood dripped from the tips of its long, sharp horns. Its gaze settled on the two boys. As it paced hungrily toward them, the sorcerer snickered and clutched the disk. "Yes, far, far too late."

"Maybe not!" Calling upon his failing strength, Jason pushed Steve to one side and screamed, "Jump!" The boys leaped forward, then rolled under the cumbersome beast's outstretched arms. Back on his feet, Jason raced to the computer.

The sorcerer turned toward him and leveled his pointed finger at the boy. "Get away from there!"

Ignoring him, Jason ripped another disk from his pocket and jammed it into the slot. As he quickly worked the keyboard, a bolt of blue light flashed from the sorcerer's finger. With the last of his strength, Steve hurled himself across the room, smashed into the sorcerer and sent him reeling to the ground. The off-target bolt crackled outward, pulverizing the howling half-man, half-monster in a blast of flame and smoke.

Once again, Jason hit the DELETE command, and the lock vanished once more. Next, with the touch of a final key, the SAVE command flashed onto the screen. This time a gust of air rushed upward. The boys each felt something warm and strong seeping into them as they watched the sorcerer begin to fade.

"How?" the conquered being moaned weakly.

Jason held up a game disk. "The first thing I ever learned about computers was to always make a backup." Leaning over, he reached out his hand and helped Steve to his feet. By the time the boys left the room, only a pale lavender haze remained of their challenger. Outside the door, the pit, too, was disappearing. But as they squeezed under an old board and stepped into the sunshine, the haze in the darkened room began to swirl. A small spark flared within it, and at that moment, the computer screen lit up in each boy's room at home. A single message flashed at the center of each screen:

GAME OVER – PLAY AGAIN?

The Lesson

essy carefully tugged at the silver bow on the birthday present from her brother. So far it had been a great party. A dozen friends had come to help her celebrate, and she had received some really cool gifts. Still, she couldn't believe that her brother, Ted, had actually gotten her a present. He was two years older than she, and he usually spent more time trying to find ways to annoy her than to please her.

She loosened a strip of tape that held the shiny, pink paper in place and slipped out a tall, black tube. "What is it?" She looked into her brother's eyes, searching for signs of a gag.

"Open it, and you'll find out." Ted smiled innocently.

Jessy twisted the top. It was snug, so she gave it a very hard turn. Suddenly, the top flew out of her hands, and the package seemed to explode. A half-dozen, cloth-covered "snakes" sprang into the air, and confetti rained down on everyone.

Jessy and a few of the guests screamed and covered their eyes. When she finally peeked through her fingers, she could see that everyone was laughing. Ted, however, was not simply laughing; he was rolling on the floor. He was howling so hard that tears streamed down his cheeks.

"Thanks a lot, Ted." Jessy turned down one corner of her mouth the way she always did when she was angry with her brother.

"You . . . you. . . . " He struggled to speak between guffaws. "I can't believe you fell for that. I didn't think anybody was that stupid! You are so gullible."

Jessy just scowled. She felt her face grow warm with embarrassment. Ted never seemed to care how he hurt her feelings.

By early evening the guests had gone home, and Jessy was in the kitchen helping her mother tidy up. She stepped on the small pedal at the base of the plastic trash bin, and the lid popped open. When she had been very little, Ted had told her that the top only opened when the bin was hungry and wanted to be fed. To prove his point, he had asked her to step closer, and when the lid suddenly sprang up, he'd grabbed her wrist and tried to put her hand inside as she struggled and screamed.

For days, Ted taunted her with the vicious trash bin that seemed to snap ravenously at her. She had believed him until she finally caught him pressing the pedal down with the back of his heel. Ever since then, it seemed that Ted never missed an opportunity to tease her and make her feel dumb.

The memory made her angry again as she tossed in a handful of crumpled birthday paper and let the lid slam shut. "Mom," Jessy tilted her head, "what does gullible mean?"

"Well, if someone is gullible, they can be easily tricked or misled," her mom answered. "Why?"

"Oh, nothing." She turned away so that her mother couldn't see her expression. "The party would have been perfect if Ted hadn't tried to ruin it," Jessy announced sullenly.

Her mom's voice was filled with concern. "Why do you say that? You know he only teases you."

"That's what everyone says, but its more than just teasing. He's mean. I wish he wasn't my brother!"

"Jessy! That's a terrible thing to say. I know you think he picks on you, but you probably do things that annoy him, too. You'd be much better off if you tried to get along."

"I'm going to put my gifts in my room now." Jessy headed for the family room. Her mother just didn't understand. She threw her new sweater over her arm and gathered up the stack of books and games that had been piled onto the coffee table.

Once in her room, she closed the door. Without turning on the light, she put the stack on her dressing table and flopped across her bed. Easily tricked, she thought. Well, I won't let him trick me again . . . ever! I'd give anything to teach him a lesson just once.

Jessy was still brooding when she heard the tapping on

the window beside her bed. At first she thought it might be a branch moving in the wind, but then she heard her name whispered very softly. The voice was coming from just under her windowsill. Jessy chewed lightly on her lower lip.

"Go away, Ted," she muttered. "I'm not falling for it this time."

The tapping continued, and the voice spoke once more. "I'm not your brother," it cooed. Slowly, Jessy rolled over and stood. The moon was full, and she could easily see through the window into the backyard. The old swing set shimmered in the silvery light and one swing stirred gently in the light breeze, but that was all. She began to turn away.

"Come closer," the voice urged. Jessy froze. Her eyes grew wide as she frantically looked around for the source of the strange voice. "Come closer, and I will show myself to you."

Jessy wanted to scream, to turn and run, but instead she stepped slowly toward the window. She felt her feet move almost as if they had a will of their own. She drew closer and pressed her trembling fingertips against the windowpane. Then she saw it, crouched directly under the sill. It didn't look at all human. Whatever it was leered back at her with dreadful yellow eyes. Its stooped body was covered with long, greasy-looking hair from head to foot. Jessy was riveted to the spot.

The creature spoke. "Don't let my appearance fool you," it hissed. "I'm here to help you." It spread its mouth in a ghastly grin, turned up its hands and shrugged. She could see that its long, gnarled fingers ended in sharp talons.

"H-h-how . . . how could you help me?" Jessy stammered. She felt the hair stand up on the back of her

neck. "I don't want you to help me. Go away!" Her voice rose to a shriek.

"Shhh," the beast soothed. "You said you would give anything to teach your brother a lesson, didn't you? Well, that's what I'm here for. I can show you how."

In spite of the beast's horrible appearance, it had gained Jessy's interest. The image of her brother laughing at her, making her look foolish in front of all her friends at her own birthday party, came to mind. Her fear began to turn to cautious curiosity. "What do you mean?"

"Open the window and I will tell you," it coaxed. "Together we will teach your brother a very important lesson."

Jessy stared at the monster. It looked back at her, urging, encouraging; its glowing, lemon-colored eyes were hypnotic. Uncertainly, she reached toward the window latch, then snatched her hand away. "No, I'm afraid."

"Don't be. I won't hurt you. We are going to teach your brother a lesson. You won't regret it."

Suddenly, her bedroom door swung open, and the room was flooded with light from the hall. "Who are you talking to?" Ted demanded.

Jessy snapped her head around to see his dark shape in the doorway. "Look out the window!" she yelled. "Quick, there's a monster under the windowsill outside." Ted hesitated. "Look!" she insisted. "It's right outside."

He moved to the window and looked out, his back to her. Then he turned around. With a glassy stare he raised his arms and began to shuffle stiffly toward her. "Yes, master, I will obey," he moaned.

"Don't, Ted." Jessy backed away, but her brother coldly closed the gap between them. He stretched out his fingers and reached for her neck. His eyes rolled upward. His lip wrinkled into a hideous sneer, and a low growl sounded deep in his throat.

"Don't, Ted. Stop or I'll scream!" Her voice was rising.

Ted dropped his hands and laughed. "You are such a dope. There's nothing out there. I've got better things to do than play with a stupid scaredy-cat." Making meowing noises, he sauntered out of her room, closing the door behind him.

As the darkness closed in, Jessy heard the voice whisper, "We could teach him a lesson he'll never forget."

Jessy didn't turn. She bunched her hands into tight fists and simply asked, "How do I know I can trust you?"

There was a moment of silence, then the beast spoke. "I will give you a demonstration."

"How will I know what it is?" Jessy said.

"You'll know," it hissed.

· · · · · · · · · ·

At breakfast the next morning, Ted asked Jessy if it was safe to go outside or if there was a monster hiding under the front porch. During lunch at school, he loudly told several of his friends the story, and they all found opportunities to embarrass her about it. Everyone thought it was particularly funny when she pulled a small can out of her lunch bag and it turned out to be cat food. Gleefully, Ted announced that even scaredy-cats had to eat. Jessy was fuming, but in the light of day, she was beginning to doubt her story herself. By the time she was on her way home, she had convinced herself that it was all a dream.

They lived only four blocks from school, so Jessy and her brother rode their bikes each day. Today Ted hadn't met her at their usual place, so she decided to wheel her bike along as she walked home with her friend Alice. The girls were deep in conversation and didn't notice a slight rustling in the hedge beside them. When they reached the corner, Ted and two friends charged out from the bushes. "Monster attack!!" they howled.

Jessy squealed and dropped her bike. Her books scattered on the sidewalk. "Ted, you creep!" She was almost in tears. "I'll get you for this! Leave me alone!"

Hooting and laughing, the boys raced for their bikes, which were hidden behind the hedge. Ted began to pedal as fast as he could, but before he had traveled a few feet, the front wheel of his bike twisted as if something strong had yanked it toward the hedge. Ted flew off and sprawled across the sidewalk. His pants ripped at the knee, and his notebook landed in the muddy trickle of water that flowed in the gutter.

"It serves you right, Ted!" Alice yelled.

Jessy didn't say anything. She simply stared at the dark, razor-clawed hand that slid back into the shadows of the hedge.

• • • • • • • • • •

That night she sat in her darkened room, waiting. She knew that it was wrong to wish harm on her brother, but he had always been so mean to her. Besides, he hadn't really been hurt. All she wanted to do was teach him a lesson. Maybe then he would try to be nicer to her. The sound of the monster's hiss startled her.

"Did you like my little demonstration?" it whispered.

"Yes," Jessy barely breathed. "What are you going to do next?"

"Open the window, and we will make our plans together."

Jessy leaned toward the window and looked down into a pair of yellow eyes that glittered evilly in the moonlight. "If you're so smart, why don't you open the window yourself?"

She thought she heard a low, angry snarl, but the monster soon answered. "I cannot reach you unless you make the first move."

Once again Jessy reached for the latch. "You promise you won't hurt me?" she asked.

"I promise," it replied.

"With all your heart," she added.

"With all my heart," it agreed.

Jessy grasped the latch, and this time she turned it. The wood creaked as she pushed the window open and leaned out to listen. Without warning, the monster leapt toward her, gripped her throat with its long, bony fingers and snatched her off her feet. It was unnaturally strong. She tried to scream, but it was cutting off her air. Her legs and arms beat helplessly against the creature's slimy hide.

"You promised you wouldn't hurt me," she gasped. "You promised with all your heart. We were going to teach my brother a lesson."

She could feel the monster's hot, rancid breath as it pulled her closer. "I have no heart," it growled. "And his turn will come. Now that you have opened the window of your own free will, I can enter your home as I wish. Don't worry, I will visit every member of your family before this night is over." Jessy felt the sharp talons dig deeper into her throat as the beast's mouth turned up in a horrid grin and the moonlight glistened on its dripping fangs. "You said you would give anything to teach your brother a lesson," the grotesque creature sneered. "Well, my dear, my price is quite high, and it is time to pay up." The last sound Jessy heard was that of the vile monster licking its lips.